Home Everywhere

Home Everywhere

A trip, with stories

Megan McNamer

Black
Lawrence
Press

www.blacklawrence.com

Executive Editor: Diane Goettel
Cover Design: Zoe Norvell
Book Design: Amy Freels
Compass image by StockUnlimited

Published 2018 by Black Lawrence Press.
Printed in the United States.

Philosophy is really homesickness,
an urge to be at home everywhere.
—Novalis

For my mother

Prologue

Inside a hangar at the lonely airport on the edge of her childhood town there was a small, turquoise-colored plane. It waited there in the shadows, a dragonfly at rest, a cooled moth. One summer the plane emerged, and up she went in this odd creature with her brothers and sisters, battened in for a tour of the checkerboard land. It was Fun Days in Arboleda.

The primitive hand-cranking of the propeller was impressive, and then—the roar. The plane became an activated animal, an insect, a driven intelligence. But minutes after takeoff the sky closed in, the earth seemed to rush up, she felt pressed between the two. The plane circled back and deposited her onto the airstrip, where she wobbled over to the edge and sat down.

She pressed her fingers into the warm, black pebbles melded together in the tarmac. The wind stroked the rattling grass and behind this curtain of sound she heard the plane intone... what? An ant wended its way between her fingers and across her hand. She heard the hiss of an August grasshopper, the punctuating snap.

There was the ant's private city of glistening pebbles, the tiny terra firma. There was the abandoned plane with its fragile occupants, high up in the empty sky. The pebbles and the ant and the plane all belonged to the blue-domed world. But only because she had been set down there on that dry land, on that particular day, at that one spot.

I.

I.

M(r). Butterfly

His real name was something else. It had tones and diphthongs and unaspirated p's. It was piquant and fluttering, the way he pronounced it, his voice guarded, clandestine. Quickly then he reverted to the businesslike "Ron," a created character, clearly. Ron was a combination of police, priest, parent, and pimp.

"Get into the temple," Ron might say, his language pragmatic and unadorned.

Everyone liked him.

It was nearing the end of the millennium, in the waning days of November, the waxing days of December, the darkening days of winter, the holiday season in the Western world. Time to flee the festive hearth and set off for a ten-day trip to a foreign land. (A reprieve of sorts, this bargain tour, from states of longing, aloneness, and relentless cheer.)

When they first shuffled down the chute upon arrival, they arranged their faces to say: *We are well-traveled people and students of culture.* Some made their faces say even more: *I have slept in the rainforest canopy. I have rubbed shoulders with shamans. I don't tour, I trek. I have trekked to places never before seen by the common traveler.*

The tourists knew that they were just tourists.

I have observed factory workers amid the clang of their toil. I have studied the courtship songs of refugees. I have gone right into the homes and made friends for life!

There stood the beaming Ron outside baggage claim, wearing a crisply-laundered white shirt with thin green stripes, a small brass name tag centered neatly on the pocket. His smile, which appeared to be absolutely genuine, was also instantly, guilelessly flirtatious.

"My name is R-O-N," he said, pointing with his left index finger to invisible letters in the air, a large sliver watch glinting on his wrist like a signal mirror.

"Ron!" the tourists responded, a bit precipitately.

"Ah, your English is excellent," he smiled, looking right at each of them, a flicker of irony hovering about his lips. They were made to feel good, in cahoots with Ron. He seemed to be saying: *I know, and you know, and I know you know, and I want you to know I know, and I want you to know I know you know all those clichés. About all those others. Not you.*

"Follow me," Ron chimed, and swaggered away, confident of their attention. They gathered their things and followed him, over skyways, up ramps, and around corners. They followed him to the accompaniment of "Bridge Over Troubled Water," a melancholy, duple-metered rendition strummed on a steel guitar.

(Ron had a fussy, near-prissy physical brio that exuded machismo itself, deconstructed and distilled. That was what some of the tourists noticed. Others simply noticed that his pants fit perfectly.)

Through sliding glass doors, they followed him, waddling stiff-legged after the long flight, elbowing their way out into a steamy, incubator-warm parking garage filled with growling buses waiting in the 4 a.m. neon glare at full, repressed throttle. A quick stab of travel sadness was generally experienced. Or might it be joy? They were here. None of them had been here before. A door had stood open and now it was closed and they were in. Here they were.

The only colors in the gaseous gray were purple clumps of garlands, reminiscent of leis, and the brilliant magenta of the costumes of the lei attendants, languorous, silk-swathed girls accompanied by camera-equipped boys. The sex trade! No, welcome teams. Working the arrivals.

The camera boys wore the same green stripes as Ron, though not so nattily. They stood with the girls at the open doors of the buses, an appropriate number of garlands draped over each girl's arm, brochures and tin buttons arrayed on a tray. Various toxins vied for space in the semi-enclosed area. As each panting, decompressing passenger ambled gratefully toward the steps of his (or her) designated vehicle, a girl lassoed him (or her) with a lei, saying "Welcome, Sir (or Madam)," with a quick fold of the hands to the forehead. Then the girl stood next to this perspiring, sleep-craving stranger, smooth cheek to rumpled cheek in a mini-position of intimacy, while a boy snapped a photo, redeemable later for US $10.

They wanted to be good sports about this. They wanted to seem unthreatened. They didn't always travel in hordes (they wanted this understood), but so what? They hoped to convey a stance that was not "anti," but "post." *We're beyond being ill at ease.* That was what the well-traveled hoped to convey with their stance, distinguishing themselves from the nervously beaming novices.

Everyone looked at Ron, who was monitoring the proceedings with a white, linen handkerchief kept close to his mouth and nose, presumably to filter the fumes, or maybe to dab sweat from his upper lip. Holding the folded square in place, he guided them into the bus with his free hand, the fingers performing a regular little twirl at the end of his languid arm, the heavy watch winking, the overall effect that of a blessing, a mock blessing, a tinge of carnival, a dancer moonlighting as a doorman.

They wanted to match Ron's dramatic flair. But the tourists weren't there yet. Some tried to duck the photo, others dodged the lei. A woman dropped several packages of peanuts she'd saved from the flight and also her reading glasses, which she retrieved with a pounce. This awkward behavior created a catch in the smoothness of the whole maneuver, the face of her welcome girl became knit with the faintest of frowns.

Ron came to the rescue, lowering his handkerchief and bestowing the moment with a sudden big grin, his teeth showing even and radiant in this personalized extension of his uniform smile, itself so full of pleasure and professionalism. *He exudes a male animus that an equally-short Norman Mailer would kill for,* a would-be novelist in the group made a mental note to write. *He exudes a soft concern,* thought the would-be novelist's wife. *And total authority.*

"Everything is okay?" Ron tilted his head ever so slightly. The tourists nodded mutely, eyeing the hard holster swivel clip cellphone case he had strapped to his belt, next to a black, collapsible umbrella, as compact as a billy club.

"Get into the bus," he smiled.

They did, with no further struggle.

Floating through the city and toward their beds, the tourists wondered if the cool fingers they'd felt on their arms belonged to the silky girls or to Ron. Faint sensations still lingered of just the barest moments of contact, like moths brushing skin.

Slipping into nodding half-dreams, they became the moths and Ron their captor.

Then Ron and the girls became entangled. He wore shimmering colors; they wore his name tag. Then the tourists were the ones all wrapped up with Ron. He reclaimed his name tag. It said RON. The tourists wore their own tin buttons. These said PARADISE PROMISE. As the bus sighed along, they sank fully to sleep, convinced they had finally arrived.

2.
Final Itinerary

Twenty-two hours earlier Keith described the merits of his twill pants to anyone who cared to listen. He was standing just inside the main terminal of Seattle-Tacoma International Airport at the check-in ticket counter for Oceania Airways. His pants were moisture wicking, Keith explained. Breathable and wrinkle proof. Also lightweight, he added, and "virtually indestructible." His only apparent audience was Irene, who shared with Keith a literal bent. She listened politely, then intently, as if imagining the ravages Keith's pants might be required to endure in the upcoming week.

A tall woman in the group wearing beaded bangle bracelets asked Irene if her vest was Guatemalan. Irene didn't know. They all proceeded through security, performing the obligatory small moves with a stop-start cadence, attendant facial expressions conveying nervous irritation, suppressed eagerness, and embarrassment at the occasional splayed contents of carry-on bags.

They hurried, there was a general sense that they needed to get inside quickly, even though their flight was hours away. Any dawdling might attract notice. They might be detained, or worse. They might be shot. Well, maybe not shot. Members of the group shushed each other, this was not the time to make jokes. They waited in another line to change money, gazing at posters of pagodas and

Buddha statues and golf courses, their eyes unfocused or fixed on something beyond. They pretended to be bored, to calm their hearts.

Keith outlined for Irene the varying protocols for tipping taxi drivers of the world. He said there was a big difference between the designations of "taxi-taxi" and "taxi-meter" at their particular destination. It had to do with the pay rate, the method of calculation. There was nothing straightforward about this, but certain clues would be displayed on the taxis indicating which was what. It was possible to do something or other that you would regret.

Keith had the pertinent section in his guidebook highlighted in yellow. He showed it to Irene, who produced reading glasses on a stretchy neon-green neck cord, a purchase she was already regretting. Then he showed it all around, his big hands shaking with excitement or some kind of palsy as he pushed up his own glasses and pressed the pages flat.

The woman with the beaded bangles asked Irene if her vest was Indonesian. Irene didn't know. She had bought it at the mall in Crag on the very same day she bit the bullet and booked her flight. Was it *batik? Ikat?* The woman wouldn't give up.

A husband and wife wearing identical white canvas hats shared custody of a glass-eyed teddy bear as if it were necessary baggage or a child.

"It is a remarkably long way away," the husband remarked affably to the people behind, as he recounted other trips. "I'm not quite sure from where."

Irene fumbled for her RealRoutes Chartered Quests, PARADISE PROMISE—Amazing Asia! itinerary.

Day 01. Today we span the Pacific on board Oceania Airway's 747 wide-cabin jet. Cross the international date line and lose one calendar day.

It read to her like the rules for a game. Toss the dice, center section, Row 12, Seat F. She headed toward Women, stepping around a sad-eyed man who had identified himself to the group as Pete. She and Pete hadn't yet spoken, but she wondered about his crutch.

Tourists go out looking for the dramas in their dreams. Irene bet she got that from her brother Herbert, who probably got it from a book. Probably when she and Fred were planning to go to the Grand Canyon. Fred was new then and still alive, and they borrowed his uncle's camper pickup. It hadn't worked out, though. And then Fred was dead, before she'd hardly gotten used to him.

Irene liked dramas full of mystery and brooding and English accents. Grimly shouldering a rucksack, climbing the steps of a prop jet, dictating a telegram. *Passage uneventful.* Stop.

"I'm going to the Ukraine," Irene might say to her cat Bisquick as she looked for her keys and grocery list. She was unclear whether it was "the Ukraine" or just "Ukraine."

"I'm off to Russia," she'd say. *Return uncertain.* Stop.

The specifics of Irene's travel fantasies would be difficult, if not downright embarrassing, to describe in conversations with humans. Running along high cliff meadows, reached by helicopter only certain times of the year. Reclining on a teak chaise on an empty patio, small breezes licking her toes. Emerging from the cool recesses of a monastery to walk in hand-hewn sandals across the baked stone. (Some of this, it was true, came from *Flyaway Magazine*.)

"Fire is by no means unusual, as the houses are mostly constructed of wood."

The man with the teddy bear was enjoying an exchange on cross-cultural arcana with his neighbors in line, who had friends who knew his wife's sister, as it turned out.

~

The passengers in first class, mostly men, though privileged immediately with plastic glasses of orange juice, seemed lonely and faintly needy up there behind the heavy, partially-closed curtains, a few already tucked up in fleecy blankets like blood donors. Irene waited for an elderly man wearing a bolo tie made from a bullet casing to get situated so she could pass. The man had a National Rifle

Association pin on the lapel of his oversized suit jacket and he wore a large tin button on his baseball cap stating: *We sleep peacefully in our beds because rough men are willing to do violence on our behalf.*

He was cautioning pale Denise, the only officially young person in the PARADISE group, about deep vein thrombosis.

"It's not the clot that'll take a guy down," said the man to Denise, who responded with the blankest of stares. "It's the clot breaking away and traveling."

He blinked at the small tattoo in the middle of Denise's forehead, nestled in among her very black, jagged hair. It was of an eye, not quite normal size, but there it was, only partly obscured by a long forelock. When he first saw that tattoo (the old man confided to himself out loud), he thought it was a head wound.

Denise stared at the man with all her eyes.

Irene gazed at the seat back in front of her. She was determined to feel the humanity all around, a feat she accomplished by burrowing into her own, focused-down world. She was happy to be surrounded by strangers, who would likely remain strange forever. A college boy with big, knobby knees, traveling alone, that was good. Sad-eyed Pete, with his crutch. A Korean couple with a baby, fine, fine. She loved them all, even if the Korean couple had four, spilling, carry-on bags between them, not one of which seemed to contain whatever it was they wanted.

The college boy sneezed loudly into his hands, several times in succession, saying "damn," instead of "excuse me." The Korean man and wife did not speak to Irene in any recognizable language as they set up camp in their designated seats, nor she to them. Instead, they smiled at one another and murmured meaningless, made-up syllables. Expressions of good will.

Everyone agreed to avoid touching no matter what.

~

"This aircraft is at least thirty years old."

A voice buried somewhere in the mass of passengers could be heard sharing this unwelcome information. The passengers pretended to be aloof, donning the mask of the dispassionate traveler.

"All these aging aircraft will need to be retired in the next five years."

In preparation for its long march forward, the drink cart passed to the rear of the plane. Except for the spotty first class, the plane was full. There was a backlog in departures, one runway unusable, no explanation why. The drink cart was set into forward motion, even though the plane was still.

"The number three engine separated from the fuselage."

The doomsday voice had launched into a story. Irene brought forth possible beverage orders for consideration. Orange juice? A Pepsi product? She was trying to decide what someone such as herself might like to drink. She had her airplane blanket handy for nap time, her carry-on safely stowed, a pleasant half-smile at the ready. She turned to sad Pete with the crutch. Dreadful to have a disability. The poor man had been waylaid for a bit, two uniformed airport personnel tracing patterns in the air with metal-detecting wands. No real laying on of hands, just the most hesitant of pats.

Irene wondered at Pete's decision to join a tour group of able-bodied travelers. She patted her reading glasses, hanging folded over her heart, and traced her hairline with her ring finger, careful not to touch her actual face or hair. She was thinking to begin a conversation. She thought she'd talk a bit about Seattle, the fish market and so on. She wanted to talk about where they were going, too, the people, the culture. Pete looked out the window. His crutch was deposited in the overhead bin, traded for two airplane pillows, which he wedged tightly up against the armrest that separated him from Irene.

The teddy bear couple was settled in the row behind, the bear between them. Irene noted that they addressed each other formally, as Mr. and Mrs. Small. She could hear them arguing in a good-natured way. The topic seemed to be exploration and warfare.

"Guns, germs, and steel, Mr. Small," said Mrs. Small, taking off her canvas hat and fluffing her well-cut, graying hair. "I'm certain of it!"

Irene wondered if the teddy bear carried by Mr. and Mrs. Small was akin to a stuffed bear once featured in her local newspaper, the *Arboleda Pioneer*. The bear was sponsored by Mrs. Dickinson's fourth-grade classroom at Arboleda Elementary. His name was Dudley. He went the forty miles to the Crag Airport with Ted Johnsrud, who was going to Denver for his sister and brother-in-law's 25th wedding anniversary. Ted was to hand off the bear there to someone else, just any old someone. There were pre-addressed postcards tucked into Dudley's vest pocket and a note instructing his arbitrary custodians to contact Mrs. Dickinson's class with reports of his adventures and to keep Dudley moving.

"The Travels of Dudley" eventually appeared in the *Pioneer*'s "On the Go" page, with photos of Dudley pre-departure, and close-ups of notes received from South Carolina, Finland, Rome, Melbourne, and Tahiti. Dudley went off the radar somewhere over the Pacific.

Irene relayed all this information in a confidential tone to Pete, who was nonresponsive. Well (she continued anyway), maybe the Smalls' bear wasn't a round-the-world bear at all. Maybe he was just a stuffed bear with no special status.

"The black box didn't show up, even with Navy seals."

The purveyor of disaster was the elderly man with the bullet casing bolo tie. His voice was unusually loud, perhaps because he wore a malfunctioning hearing aid, a fact he had divulged to the occupants of several rows of seats.

"It was terrorist bombs destroyed the U.S. embassies in Kenya and Dar es Salaam," he informed the flight attendant, as he moved on to other stories of calamity. She beamed and handed him a plastic-wrapped headset.

~

Safe-T-Man had Irene's attention. Safe-T-Man was a handy companion for women on the road. Irene adjusted her reading glasses and smoothed the pages of SkyMall. Thoughts of Arboleda had stirred a disquiet in her mind, something akin to homesickness, with dark, hollow musings. An inflatable life-sized simulated male, Safe-T-Man could serve as a guard against all the bad things that—who knows?— might happen to women traveling alone.

She liked the nonchalant way he wore his mirrored sunglasses, leather jacket, and billed cap. The overall effect was one of easy competence. He could be a driving instructor. Or a professional assassin.

She decided to request one of those little bottles of Chardonnay to go with her snack mix. But then a flight attendant plopped an ice cream bar onto her lowered tray. Unasked for. Everyone was getting one. The plane seemed to be stalled and was getting uncomfortably warm. Irene looked at this already-melting offering and thought: Oh well. (*Submit.*) She fumbled in her nylon shoulder bag and swallowed dry a Sudafed. She decided she would have a cup of tea instead, for now, whenever the drink cart arrived.

The plane was not moving, it was just panting in place, like an enormous pet.

"It broke into three pieces and burst into flame." The man with the bolo tie had found a cordial listener, a teenage boy wearing ear buds. The boy plucked a bud out of an ear at periodic intervals, nodded without comprehension, and laughed a little, reluctantly showing his braces.

Menus were circulated. There were two dinner choices, beef or sole. The rest was simply information about what would come. Irene read the words carefully, as if the menu were a program. Garden fresh salad. San Francisco sourdough roll with sweet-cream Almost Butter. Slowly she peeled the soggy wrapper from her ice cream treat. The Korean couple across the aisle did likewise, speaking quietly to each other and to their spike-haired baby, who was lolling out into the aisle, his head precariously in the path of any drink cart that might come. The baby took one lick of the ice cream and fell soundly asleep. His eyelashes looked like centipedes crossing his cheeks.

Many minutes passed, apologies periodically squawked in fits over the loudspeaker, the pilot's words as jumbled and slurred as a middle-schooler's. This was especially true when he tried to pronounce "turbulent conditions." Irene remarked to Pete, her manner scrupulously off-hand, that the pilot sounded very relaxed. Pete didn't answer, but he nodded his assent. She said that the pilot sounded almost as if he were lying down. Pete didn't respond. Maybe she just imagined saying that last thing. It was something her brother Herbert might say. (*Is he fucking lying down?*)

Video screens spaced regularly throughout the cabin burst into color with welcoming safety lessons. They blipped off, then stuttered back on. The plane's electronic equipment was gathering itself together into a coalesced plan of forward-go. The safety lessons, it occurred to more than one person, had arrived early. The plane still hadn't moved. A flight attendant mimed a loose interpretation of the video's message, her motions stiff but dreamy, a cheerleader under water. Irene pictured all the plane's occupants under water, clinging to their seat cushions, kicking up, up, up to the sunlight, their cheeks puffed out like cartoons.

A clutch of Unitarians lifted plastic glasses full of ice and fizzy beverages. They had been served their drinks and were performing a quiet toast, desiring some small ritual, but reluctant to distinguish themselves from travelers less merry.

"Cheers!" Keith called to them across the seats, in support of their camaraderie.

"Prost!" responded a Unitarian.

"Skal!" someone else joined in.

"Salud!" People began to laugh.

"Hipahipa!"

This last, from Mr. Small, was met with silence.

"It's Hawaiian," he explained. Then he and Mrs. Small bent their heads for a private consultation.

Irene was remembering a dinner lecture in the basement community room of St. Gerald's. It had been billed as a benefit for World Hunger, but was mostly about wildlife. There was a map full of stick pins, the colored heads representing all the places toured by the featured speaker. With dinner there was a PowerPoint and with dessert there was video footage of somewhere in Africa. The footage was mostly of bushes. The guests in the community room had quietly waited for something to emerge.

"Egeszsegedre!" said the woman with the many bangle bracelets, raising an empty hand high and twirling her wrist. "Hungarian!"

The elderly man with the bolo tie pulled a glossy card from the seatback in front of him. It showed the layout of the airplane. He held it up close for examination. His hand moved to the inner pocket of his suit jacket, and he carefully circled all the exit doors with a felt-tip pen.

The drink cart finally flanked Irene. She ordered gin.

3.
Stage Fright
Irene

It happened after school, crystalline weather, the sky a vivid blue. They were standing on the corner, waiting for the light to change. A frantic, dying yellowjacket trapped in the cab of a pickup truck stung the driver, whose foot then hit the gas pedal instead of the brake. The truck slammed up onto a curb, striking both children. The daughter died instantly. The son was flown to Seattle's Harborview Hospital, where he died later that day. Irene's neighbor and childhood acquaintance, Mrs. Howard (Tina) Cunningham, was the mother in this story.

Tina was on her mind, but the accident wasn't really an appropriate story for sharing with newly-met travel companions. The day prior to departure from SeaTac Irene stopped for a quick visit to drop off her house key before heading back across the street in the first snowfall of the season to wait for her ride to the Crag airport. She was scheduled to take Horizon Air to Seattle and spend a night in the SeaTac Marriott. And then: the beginning of her trip, her Chartered Quest, her PARADISE PROMISE.

Tina would pick up Irene's newspaper and mail while she was gone. Tina was always home now.

It was the day after Thanksgiving, exactly one year, two months, three days, and some odd hours after the accident. Irene listened again to the detailed, agonized explanation of how her neighbor had requested her children to return a movie to the video store, she had even lectured them about late charges. She had urged them to walk— they should walk more, she had said, why was she always driving them around? *Her* mother hadn't driven *her* around when she was 9 and 10 years old, why was she driving them around all the livelong day? She'd had the beginning of a migraine, maybe it was the red wine she and Howard had tried the night before, to get out of their rut. She said the children should stick together, hold hands, since, although only five blocks away, the store was farther than they'd ever ventured from home alone. It would be dinnertime soon. She said they should hurry up and go.

If she had not sent them on that errand, just then, they would not have been at that particular corner at that exact moment, and they would not have been hit. They would be alive, still alive. If she had not drunk the red wine, she would not have had a migraine and would have been more amenable to driving. If she had married before her late thirties, these children, *these miracles!* would not have been quite so young and unaware as they set out obediently on that day. (If Irene's brother Herbert had not seemed to have his eye on her back in high school, she would not have waited so long before settling on Howard.) If she had not said "hurry up," the truck might have missed them. But she had, and it didn't, and they were gone.

An investigation showed that the driver was not speeding nor driving under the influence of alcohol or illegal drugs, and the county could not show he was "acting in a grossly negligent manner," a requirement for the felony charge of negligent homicide, and it wouldn't have mattered anyway, such a charge, for, as the judge said, "It's a situation where we're not ever going to come up with a happy ending."

It was not the driver's fault. He made it happen, but it was not his fault. Or it was his fault, but he didn't make it happen. Either way. Gone.

Irene sat with Tina, this neighbor and long-time acquaintance, younger sister of a classmate ("friend," yes, that too, everyone was friends in Arboleda, due to a scarcity of people). They sat in a darkened living room, shades pulled, gazing at the lights of a dark green plastic resin Christmas tree that was decorated with cellophane-wrapped candy canes. She had a tree just like it in her own living room. You could put them up early, being plastic. Hank's Hardware in Crag got in a bunch. Real trees were hard to come by in nearly treeless Arboleda and surrounding environs. The families of Irene and Tina had always decorated fake trees. Nothing had changed, nothing, the candy canes confirmed it.

Irene knew she should focus on the lost children, whose large, glossy photos flanked the gas fireplace. But she felt instead a twinge of grief for herself, foremost, and, secondarily, for Tina (now Mrs. Cunningham), for their happy, mindless, childhood selves, the kids of Arboleda, so busily constructing a safe and hopeful world, oblivious to the sorrow already in store. She noticed that someone had stenciled spray-foam snowflakes onto Tina's living room window for a cozy effect, and they clung there, even as real snow fell through the morning darkness outside, gathering on the window ledges and sticking to the panes.

Irene tried to think of words of comfort, but all that arose were words of fate, words garnishing a Sunday bulletin at St. Gerald's recently, with no accompanying explanation.

The paper reeds by the mouth of the brook shall wither, be faded away, and be no more.

(It was the new priest. The old priest, by his own description, had been more of a cup-half-full kind of guy.)

Irene and Tina—who as a child had been famous for her two-fingered whistle and liked to pretend she was a small horse, galloping to school and cantering back—were now middle-aged, Irene older by several years. Which Irene could not believe. Tina didn't care. Tall, teenage girls, visiting nieces, slouched in and out of the room in low-slung jeans, their tender navels flashing discretely. The girls stared furtively at the two women, who, in turn, stared at the decorated tree in the corner of the room. Tina, one year, two months, three days, and some odd hours after the accident, without making a sound or touching her face, wept.

At that very moment, a man walked up the aisle of a nearly-full, morning rush hour Seattle city bus, pulled out a gun, and fired. He shot twice at the driver, who wrenched the steering wheel to pull the bus across two lanes of traffic, braking as he died. Then the gunman shot himself in the head as the bus became launched. It sailed off the Aurora bridge, briefly airborne, then crashed onto an apartment building, fifty feet below. One passenger died instantly, many were grievously injured. Some walked away.

As Irene's Horizon Air flight tentatively lowered itself into greater Seattle's sea of lights, the pavement all along Fremont Avenue still sputtered with flares. On the TV news at the SeaTac Marriott the flares looked faintly liturgical, even festive. Irene unwound with a gin and tonic, after taking full advantage of the bathroom amenities, the tea tree shampoo and conditioner, the tiny vial of body lotion, and she thanked her lucky stars she hadn't had to take any buses.

Falling off the world. Those were the words Irene's brother Herbert found to describe death, when he was only three. He was regarding an antelope, dead and hanging out in the machine shed, waiting to be skinned. It was October in Montana, hunting season, dead deer and antelope adorned the land. Maybe he was thinking of the antelope alive and upright, springing head up through the fields. And then the antelope was inverted, hanging from a rafter, its legs splayed as if it were plummeting.

The face comes off. Herbert said that, too, as he watched Dad butcher the animal.

~

Irene was known in the community as a singer. She rarely did solos anymore though, not since an unfortunate incident at the Lions

Club. That phrase, Herbert's *falling off the world*, came to mind whenever she thought of the incident, which wasn't often, or at least she tried not to. It was no big deal, just stage fright, good Lord, horrible, and also ridiculous. A sudden self-consciousness, and a dizzy feeling too, like you might topple right over. The person suffering from stage fright (Herbert once told her, as if *he'd* ever know), starts fixating on the actions and trappings of being alive. *Now I am breathing in, now I am breathing out.* She'd had to quit the new yoga class at the Arboleda Health Facility when they started saying that.

If that Lions Club luncheon had been at the regular Lions Den headquarters on Main Street it would have been fine, but because it was the quarterly, they had it in the high school multi-purpose room with the raised platform stage. She supposed some people might squeak their way across that overly-polished floor without wobbling, or feeling like everyone was just seeing if you would make it, Mrs. Dickinson already seated at the piano. You'd think she'd swilled the gin she'd only sipped, a pre-prandial tonic because she was getting a cold. Something sure wasn't working right.

She was supposed to sing "Black is the Color of My True Love's Hair," and all she could get out was the opening. "Black...black...bl aaacckk..." Why hadn't she brought her music? Why did they have to turn off the overheads and fire up that makeshift spotlight like it was dinner theater instead of Saturday afternoon? She had to fight back an urge to dance a stiff jig, or laugh foolishly, or utter an inappropriate, even terrible, word. Jump off the mini-stage, maybe, dive, head first, into the audience, like the kids on TV. Those old fools. The Lions, she meant. She could have shrieked "We're all gonna die!" and you'd have thought she had, the way everyone looked so uncomfortable. She just didn't know what happened, why she kept opening her mouth after the "blacks," with nothing coming out. Mrs. Dickinson must have played the intro over three times. And then she got to laughing. Irene did, not Mrs. D., who looked like a little scared rabbit, good gosh, as if singing for the Lions was Oscar night.

Truth be told, after that crazy clenching she had felt sort of excited. Laughing away, all the Lions just sitting there, until she got a bit teary and Mr. Torgersen thanked her and led her off the stage and thanked everyone for coming.

She explained that she was on Benadryl, and it all blew over, no one ever brought it up anyway. And she felt that she had learned an important lesson, which was: If you get too close to the scary edge you will feel a pull and you have to ignore it and if you don't it is like there is this crazy, cock-eyed power and it has its own sort of force field and it can suck you in. It is the power to wreck things.

It's all just hanging by a thread. A gazillion shoes, ready to drop. Shoot. Those kids. They set out on a simple errand and are killed. Random, of course, pure chance, but maybe not. Maybe it was *inevitable*. Maybe their deaths were sitting, invisible, on that corner from the very days of their births. The kids rode by the spot in the car with their mother, and no one saw them.

No one saw the deaths, just sitting there.

~

Nosing its near-obsolete cockpit toward the point of full throttle, the wide-body aircraft, a gargantuan plane, roared, quieted, swung blindly around, and glided across the tarmac. Irene hastily raised her tray to its upright and locked position. She wondered what was to be done with her ice cream wrapper and where was her gin, not to mention Pete's Bloody Mary? The drink cart was suddenly in full retreat, its operations suspended.

The plane performed a full-body shimmy. It was carrying 57,825 gallons of fuel. Overhead compartments rattled, and melodious tinkling noises emanated from the service area. The plane lurched, then halted, like a runner jumping the gun.

The Korean baby woke up, his spiky shoots of hair making him look angry. He stared fixedly at Irene over his pacifier. An overhead door flopped open, hands appeared, it was quickly fastened. Only past experience told the passengers that they weren't back in the blocks, that the lurch soon would be followed by another roar, that the plane, in fact, was about to take off.

Irene, Keith, Pete, Mr. and Mrs. Small with their teddy bear, the tall woman with the beaded bracelets, the three-eyed Denise, the elderly man with the bullet casing bolo tie, the Korean couple with the baby, the teenager with braces, the college boy with knobby knees, the cheerleader flight attendants, the sleepy pilot, the lonely men in first class. They all had agreed to fling themselves to the other side of the world. They all had agreed to be flung.

A few people glanced out the window at the rain while the plane lumbered steadily down the runway. They spotted their gaze on discernible pieces of landscape, as if this tracking were necessary to keep the plane on course. A roof line . . . a roof line . . . some distant trees. . . . The passengers in the center section, far from any windows, simply sat there, trusting they were in motion.

The plane slowed and braked again, then wheeled heavily one more time, turning west toward the East. It gave a last roar, sustaining it, like a creature with its mouth open. Then it moved forward, fast.

The now alert baby blinked at Irene. She blinked back. *You have to imagine the takeoff,* she said to the baby with her eyes. *You have to picture the plane easing through the clouds and into the open sky.*

"There was no distress call." The old man turned toward the teenager as the plane pulled away from the earth. "The weather was fine."

They had agreed not to scream. Just as people on soothing, rock-a-bye Ferris wheel rides agree to smile, broadly, and whoop, sedately, as they all go round and round.

~

Irene could see the tilted face of the strange tattooed girl over by a window, her third eye staring up at nothing. She saw the baby's bare foot pressed against his mother's thigh, fingers circling his ankle. *There is nothing to be done,* the engines soothed, *nothing to be done, noth-*

ing to be done. They were at 20,000 feet now and climbing, jetting out over the silver ocean. The Fasten Seatbelt sign remained on as the plane worked its way upward. Occasional thumps and thuds could be felt, as if large animals were in the baggage compartment fighting.

"There were suggestions it broke up mid-air."

Irene thought about the bus careening from the bridge, breaking through the day, taking flight. In a small corner of her mind she wondered about the airplane's pilot, and the co-pilot, smooth-cheeked youths both; she'd seen them when boarding, just a glimpse. She wondered if there might have been some moment during takeoff when one or the other said to himself—*No. Don't do it.*

Then she tried not to wonder.

4.
Arrival

The plane landed, bumping hard, its reassuring drone expanding to a shuddering roar. Alfred and Iris presented their faces to each other inquiringly. They obeyed the instructions to stay seated, not even moving to gather themselves together, as some passengers were doing. They seemed to have sat for the entire trip staring straight ahead, not speaking, Alfred with his hands folded over his bright, striped t-shirt, Iris keeping her new tote bag close at hand, their tin PARADISE PROMISE buttons positioned squarely. No inflatable neck pillows, no eye masks, no movie headphones, not even any reading material. All through the flight Alfred and Iris simply sat, like a couple in a large clinic. They sat waiting for their appointment with Asia.

Alfred and Iris were thinking of quitting the Presbyterians, but they weren't ready for the Unitarians. They had agreed to join the Unitarian group on the Asian Studies package tour in response to urging from Alfred's second cousin Joe, who said he and Eunice were going, but then, as it turned out, Joe and Eunice didn't go, and, as it also turned out, Alfred and Iris weren't even with the Asian Studies group, they were with this PARADISE PEEKABOO crowd or some damn thing. That dingbat at Fly-By-Night travel, or whatever it was called, some damn thing. She signed them up for the wrong damn thing!

The PARADISE gang was a mixed bunch. Alfred had been afraid they might be wild party people, but, in the flesh, that didn't seem likely. Some flashed day-of-the-week pill dispensers, then secreted these away in their fanny packs. At least two confessed they had heart conditions. Keith had those shaking hands, Pete had a false leg. Everyone filed past Pete into the travel pod during the refueling stop at Narita Airport. The travel pod was a kind of temporary resting leaf a concourse or two away from the main terminal; its hollow veins funneled the passengers in from the ozone. Pete headed to the Plexiglas smoking cell, unhurried but dogged, using his crutch and pacing himself.

They want to be out here in the world, these fragile travelers. Irene was hearing Herbert again, the Herbert in her head, reading from some book, singing some silly tune, writing his goofy poetry, painting them all with his crazy invisible brush. *Time is short, and they want to see what they can see. Oh-ho-say, can you seeee? They reach for experience like it's oxygen! sunlight! nicotine!*

Irene was enjoying her travel clothes. She wore a cotton/linen dress over her compression stockings. The dress was mid-calf, drab brown, and she wore with it the short, embroidered vest. She was privately pleased with this outfit. She got it at Agape, the new store in the Crag Mall, with the wood floors and free mini cups of herbal tea. The skirt material was crinkly and crimped, "for an airy, transcendent texture," according to the cursive description that had been attached with coarse twine. Irene imagined that her outfit evoked the layered dress of some sort of religious person. She had no idea why she had bought the neon-green glasses cord, except that it seemed handy, the way it could be zipped open and used as a secret case. She couldn't think what to zip inside it, but the feature pleased her anyway.

Some of the younger passengers carried their passports in cloth carriers around their necks like oversized Catholic scapulars. Irene carried hers in the zipped inner pocket of her nylon carry-on, which also contained a fleece sweater, an inflatable neck pillow purchased at SeaTac, destined never to leave its plastic wrapper, and a paperback she'd picked up at her First Wednesday book exchange, *Emma*, by Jane Austen, the actress Gwyneth Paltrow pictured on the cover. Where Irene left off, Emma's very good opinion of Frank Churchill *was a little shaken. . . . He was gone off to London merely to have his hair cut. A sudden freak seemed to have seized him at breakfast . . . there was an air of foppery and nonsense in it which she could not approve.*

This was slow going. She should have gone with the Sue Grafton. *N is for Noose.*

~

Keith hoisted a teardrop-shaped Gore-Tex satchel that he explained to the others (several times) was ergonomically designed to distribute weight in such a way that the wearer would not become stooped, but he was. Stooped. Sort of oppressed-looking, observed Mrs. Small to Mr. Small. Yes, a stance of weary despondence, Mr. Small agreed. Like Willy Loman.

They snuggled into the comfy reclining seats of the tour bus.

"Everyone is okay?"

The tired PARADISE PROMISE troupe nodded to Ron, their dapper tour guide. Some chorused "Yes!" Then they gazed out the tinted windows of the bus, staring into the eyes of their own green, reflected images. There was general smiling. Ron attended to them, passing out stubby pencils and pre-check-in cards for the Hotel New Riverview.

The lonely men in first class had been left behind, some standing by the baggage carousels in a small group, others already following placard-bearing drivers from various multi-national corporations. The college boy with the knobby knees had scrambled into a cab and gone sneezing off into the night. The Unitarians had their own Ron, whose name was Bill. They peeled off from the Arrivals pack to follow Bill. The Korean couple and their baby had not been seen since Narita. Irene followed them down the ramp there and thought about how she would never see them again. Then she forgot them forever.

Occasionally a vision of a face from the street flared into view and mingled with those reflected in the tinted windows. A woman hurried along the roadway, bent under an unidentifiable bundle. An old man leaned on a cane and peered up and down a side street. Youthful laborers—boys really—slept in the open beds of trucks the bus passed, their arms outstretched, their heads tilted back, their mouths sagged open.

Pete shoved his crutch into the space between the seat and the window, then looked out at the boys, his sad eyes becoming even sadder. The bus tipped a bit, making heads feel curiously light. This, it was tacitly agreed, was transcontinental travel: arriving bleary, spacey, disoriented, beat.

"What do you know!" the elderly man with the bolo tie said in an abrupt loud voice.

"I'll be darned," said Keith, as the bus passed a bright establishment with a sign that read *Internet Café*.

"Good," exclaimed Irene to no one in particular, in response to Ron's interesting fact, shared over a microphone, part of a pattering monologue, that his country had never once waged war.

Is this a snippet of real life or a demo? Herbert whispered in her ear, and she couldn't help wondering.

Irene wanted to know about things, she wanted to contribute to conversations on a regular basis. Maybe even write interesting articles for the *Arboleda Pioneer*. (An idea she divulged to no one.) The nature of the world we live in.

Pete did not share the fact with anyone that he had never flown before. He rubbed his face with one hand and looked out at the streaming neon and at the dim shapes of buildings beyond. All that fuss on the plane with the cumbersome drink cart, the rhythmic scoop of the ice, the inquiry, the selection . . . it had surprised him, that ritual. Prior to departure, the plane had been crowded, jumbled, a confusion of bags at the beginning, awkward bodies, banging plastic doors. A haphazard nervousness pervading the air. But the moment the plane's wheels left the ground the world reconfigured into what passed for an orderly scheme. The turbulence that had been predicted hours ago hadn't happened, not anything to speak of. The sense of chaos resolved itself into a kind of numb coherency as the passengers hummed along, held up by the huge engines, only them, enfolded in their grinding chant. *There is nothing to be done*, the engines soothed, *nothing to be done, nothing to be done.*

And now, after the steamy mess of the airport terminal parking lot, this silent bus. Pete felt suspicious. He was on his guard. He distrusted ritual. He'd complained a few times about this and that to the flight attendants and maybe once to Irene—how the air in the plane's cabin was too cold, how the crying babies could drive a guy nuts. But secretly he wanted everyone in the group to be uncomfortable. Why travel all over to hell and gone if all you got was happy hour? Ten days. They stretched out as far as the eye could see.

"Prior planning prevents poor performance," said the old man in the bolo tie, in response to Keith's disclosure that his camera bag was humidity-proof.

It's a fucking gulag, thought Pete, in a brief spasm of panic.

Ron patrolled the aisle.

~

Maybe it was like communion, this whole thing, this Chartered Quest, this trip. Irene was trying to come up with a good word, a description. She bowed her head and felt a wave of emotion wash over her. Communitas? Father Campana at St. Gerald's sometimes worked that word into his same-old-same-old sermons about suffering, trying to get the congregation to mix it up a little, extend a little warmth during the Kiss of Peace, which didn't usually involve a lot of kissing, everyone being Arboledians.

Irene's mind was zig-zagging with fatigue and she gave a little hiccup of mirth, then quickly covered her eyes, as if she were resting. There would be hardship, certainly. (*Pull yourself together.*) Gritty eyes, cramped legs, unsettled stomachs, fear... But all of it minor, purposeful, scheduled, and shared. (Shut up, Herbert.)

Denise looked into a little mirror and carefully powdered her tattooed eye and applied dark, chocolate-colored lipstick, smacking her lips. Anticipation was in the air, despite the general tiredness. Interest, enlivenment, a kind of quickening. Cracking a window the allowable inch, Mrs. Small felt on her arm a tiny, wing-like breath. *We're alive.* Everyone relaxed into the high-backed seats. *Still alive.* Keith leaned across the aisle and pointed out a motorcycle-taxi, his finger shaking. Hope, fraternity, a restrained kind of bliss.

At home, life was encountered solo, or in fractious families, or in lonely groups of two. (Everyone on the bus was happy to say goodbye to home.) Money was real and had to be counted, allocated, hoarded. Joints ached, offspring rebelled, pets died, mates grew peculiar, friends disappeared. And when this night reached there, in sleeping houses, the clocks would all be ticking.

"Hipahipa hooray!" called out Mr. Small, and everybody laughed.

II.

5.
The Real Mona Lisa

People gazed out the window at pond scum instead of around themselves at roped-off interior rooms full of filigree lacquer furniture, an early queen's romantic fantasy. It was Day 03 and the group was touring the current queen's summer retreat. Day 02 had been spent sleeping, arranging for extra key cards, exclaiming about the marvels of the hotel's breakfast buffet that stood available most of the morning, maintained by a cadre of young waiters who loitered by the chafing dishes in stiff suits, looking like idle groomsmen awaiting a wedding.

Part of Day 02 had been devoted to a discussion of whether it was, in fact, *not* Day 02, but rather Day 03, since the calendar had skipped a day. An air of disgruntlement hung about those who took up this position, having to do with the question of the tour's total fee, which should be reduced by the amount of one day's rate, it was reasoned, if Day 02 was not Day 02 at all.

"One dollar is a lot of money in their culture," said the elderly man with the bolo tie, which was sufficiently off the point to bring the conversation to a close.

"Excuse me, Ron. Why is it green?" Keith now asked about the pond.

"Because it is often green this way," Ron answered, which seemed to satisfy. Earlier, Keith asked Ron many questions on the bus.

"Excuse me, Ron. That grass by the side of the road. What is it called?" Keith murmured his questions hurriedly, partly in anticipation of being ignored and partly through a desire to convey the pragmatic savvy of one previously-traveled.

"Grass by the side of the road," came the cagey answer. Then Ron returned to his pattering discourse on the local language (difficult), the local people (always smiling), and the procedure at temples for using the "happy room," or bathroom (ask him, Mr. Ron).

Sometimes Ron's enigmatic replies were accompanied by a softening chuckle, at other times this was noticeably absent, such as when the elderly man with the bullet bolo tie asked, "What race are you?" out of the blue.

"Whatever is in my blood," Ron responded, raising both eyebrows ever so slightly and looking at his watch. Whether on the tour bus or here at the queen's summer palace, he was smooth and noncommittal when he was off script, whenever a question was posed directly to him. It was then as if he were a witness for this country, rather than an ambassador, a witness for the defense, giving a deposition, reluctantly.

Ron recited a continuous, nonspecific spiel about the summer palace compound, referring to it, unhelpfully, as a "compound of palace-like buildings." The group looked around, and some of them nodded. He stopped, as more and more people left the indoors to dabble their fingers in a nearby fountain.

Irene thought of a dark afternoon on a long-ago trip to Europe with her husband Fred, several years after they were married. It wasn't a second honeymoon, because there never was a first. The Grand Canyon trip never happened, things fell through. When Budget Travel in Crag advertised bargain tours to Europe, she and Fred weren't in the honeymoon mood. Fred, though, said he wanted to see the Eiffel Tower before he died. He had no idea he would die pretty darn soon. He thought he was using an expression.

Truth be told, Irene hadn't wanted any honeymoon hullabaloo anyway, when she bit the bullet and married Fred. The wedding at

St. Gerald's and church basement reception, though not cheap, had been fine, just fine. She hadn't wanted a license, either, that made it seem like hunting. It's for the children, said Dad. Children! She exclaimed. What children?

They got one, a license, it seemed impossible not to. St. Gerald's wouldn't let them marry in the church without it, and they weren't hippies, so meadows were out. The rules just took over, applying a thick, shiny shellac to the jewel of their love. Those were Herbert's words, of course. Ha ha. That had been her response.

She and Fred, except for trips to Crag and a few points not far beyond, had never really traveled together. They plodded along the hallways of the Louvre with their tour group, peering up at dimly-lit paintings, boredom lurking in the corners. Irene tried to feel something profound for the Mona Lisa when the group came upon her. She tried to extract her from all those replicas she'd seen somewhere, all the Mona Lisas of the world.

"Here she is, this is real, this is not a poster!"

Their tour guide seemed a little unstrung. When they finally left the Louvre, the skies let loose with a sudden downpour. The real Mona Lisa, to this day, was a blur, but Irene could still remember that rain. And how the look of strained concentration on Fred's face lifted, as relief came flooding in.

~

"Get into the bus ... we are going ... we are going ... get into the bus ... we are going," Ron exulted, with the measured enthusiasm of an accomplished doorway hustler.

Once everyone was seated, he greeted the group again over the microphone with a formal air, as if he had never laid eyes on any of them. He elaborated some more on a favorite theme, the king's birthday (upcoming). He touched once again on the temperament of the local people (very friendly, always smiling). He reviewed the chief characteristics of local names (long). He re-emphasized the importance of staying with the group (watch for him, Mr. Ron). He said that they were now going to visit the temple of the Jade Buddha.

"You will say 'Wow,'" Ron predicted.

And then, as the bus slowed to a crawl in the busy morning traffic, he surprised everyone by launching into a somewhat confusing story about the king's son marrying a movie star who took steroids, or perhaps the son did, or they both did. As they listened to this story, the group looked at flower-wreathed photos of the king, displayed at regular intervals along the main boulevard. In each photo the king was holding either a camera or a clarinet. Ron told a story about the king's daughter going to school in Pennsylvania and falling in love with an American.

"So now the king won't let his other children go, yup!" He wrapped it up with an almost biblical flourish. Ron finished many of his sentences with "yup," or "sure," or a conclusive "okay!" The effect was to make whatever he said seem like common knowledge, known by all the world, if not by those on the bus. Incontrovertible.

6.

The Temple

Modest garb was required for visiting the temple of the Jade Buddha. Ron told them this right after breakfast. Nevertheless, some tourists were wearing pinching shorts and sleeveless t-shirts with advertisements for shops and restaurants. Emmet Watson's Oyster Bar. The Hob Nob Café. Rockin' Rudy's, Big Al's. It could be that these t-shirts were simply comfortable, Irene thought, trying not to ignore the significance of ordinary things. It could be that they asserted a steadying influence on travelers giddy with foreignness. Maybe, too, there was something comforting about sharing this travel adventure with Big Al and Rockin' Rudy. Irene made a mental note to make an actual note, soon. Maybe the t-shirts were a way of letting the world know that those who wore them had buddies back home, that they clearly were in some groove, somewhere. But Irene noticed that people went places and then talked of nothing but other places to go. Though they didn't seem to want to hear much about Arboleda.

It was cool and shadowy inside the temple of the Jade Buddha, a nice relief after the bright, hot outdoors. Three monks, a young man and two boys, sat close to the Jade Buddha, their backs straight and their legs tucked, their bodies draped in faded russet, a velvet cord separating them from the tourists who clustered and re-clustered on the mosaic marble floor, rising and sitting with some effort, putting their legs wherever they would go.

The burden of capturing the moment had been lifted; a camcorder hung limp at Keith's side. A morose guard indicated to him that he should stow it away in its case. The guard then surveyed the bare and stockinged feet, gesturing with a liquid flick of his fingers toward those inappropriately pointing forward, and thus toward the statue of the Buddha. He waited with his hand extended in a posture symbolic of mild disapproval while the feet were laboriously arranged otherwise.

The dim stone room was filled with the rustling sounds of whispers. This was an abrupt aural change from the shouted spiels of the many tour guides outside who, with their clusters of squinting clients, wove a human chain of inquiry and documentation throughout the brilliant, gilt grounds of the Grand Palace of the King. English mixed with Italian mixed with Japanese mixed with German mixed with Chinese mixed with Dutch . . . as all learned the basic facts of the royal family and, in some cases, reminded one another of the plots, settings, and characters of *The King and I* and *Shogun* and *The Last Emperor.* Irene thought of scenes from *A Passage to India*, which she'd recently rented from Crazy Mike's Video. She remembered a mysterious echoing cave and the male lead's eyeliner.

"It's in their blood," the elderly man with the bolo tie proclaimed to perfect strangers on either side of him. When he was shushed by Mrs. Small, he stared at the mosaic floor tiles as if deciphering a code.

Mr. and Mrs. Small stood as close as they could get to the illuminated statue, hugging the wall in the soft light, Mrs. Small nudging Mr. Small forward. They wore their matching white canvas hats. Mr. Small had on a colorful Hawaiian shirt with sunsets and palm trees, and he still wore his airport lei, its blossoms bedraggled.

"Karma and rebirth," Mr. Small said at a conversational level before Mrs. Small could shush him. He carried in his backpack a small book on Buddhist philosophy that he had picked up at an English-language bookstore near the hotel.

"Is suffering caused by oneself?" Mr. Small posed this murmured question to Denise, his expression slyly quizzical. Denise scowled. She stood with her hands in the pockets of her bib overalls, gazing at the ceiling, then moved slowly away.

Pete, near the doorway, breathing hard and leaning on his crutch, did not attempt to assume any position on the floor, although he had removed his shoes, exposing his prosthesis. He wore only one sock. The others tried not to look, but did look, at his hard, fake foot, like pink stone, the nails on each toe perfect.

Keith stared attentively at the roped-off monks, as if they themselves were the featured attraction. The monks were motionless. They had been there and would be there a long time. That is how they appeared. Pete gazed at the shoulder of the monk who sat tallest. Like that of the Jade Buddha, it was bare. The human shoulder glistened with a dewy sheen.

Alfred and Iris stood near Pete, not wanting to lose the group, but hesitant to fully enter and attempt the cross-legged position. Iris had left her beige Naturalizer Walkers behind on the designated bench, but Alfred, visibly overheated, was clutching his Red Wings to his chest. They were listening to the woman with the beaded bracelets, who also hovered on the edges of the temple's interior. The woman told them that she always stood or sat near the door in public places, especially places of worship, especially in foreign lands. Since terrorism, she added, almost as an afterthought.

The breastbone of the Buddha—the historical Buddha, the human incarnation of the Buddha—was enshrined there somewhere. Irene looked at the glass-encased statue of the Jade Buddha but felt that she didn't really know what she was seeing. Her guidebook wasn't much help, making any knowledge seem a little suspect and reprimanding her with its language.

The so-called Jade Buddha, 60 cm to 75 cm high (depending on how it is measured), is actually made of a type of jasper or perhaps a low-grade nephrite, depending on whom you believe.

Ron beckoned to the group to keep moving.

7.

Get Up and Go
Keith

This wasn't Keith's first Chartered Quest. Two years prior to the PARADISE PROMISE he went on a video safari to Amazing Africa! Keith's neighbor introduced him to a gal from RealRoutes. She set it all up, with the ticket and the shots and the expedited passport.

This neighbor was concerned about Keith, who lived alone. Ever since his son's accident, Keith rarely went out. He only went to work in the afternoons at the office space he was subleasing during his semi-retirement, then to Safeway to buy something for dinner, then home. He kept this exact pattern, it was all that he could do. He didn't go to Mass at St. Catherine's anymore, he didn't go golfing, he didn't go on short drives to photograph wild flowers. He might go to Rotary on Wednesdays, but only if there was a speaker.

Sometimes Keith stood in his driveway wanting to talk. His neighbor thought that a trip with the RealRoutes people would take Keith's mind off of it. He came right out and told him so.

The safari was scheduled for April. April was the anniversary month. There had been a lot of snow pack the previous year, then a quick warming, the river had been unusually high and fast. It became muddy when it was like that. It was hard to tell just what it was doing. The surface might look slow and easy, you just didn't know.

Keith's neighbor didn't have access to much of the story, the details and all, but he had read that most suicides happen in April. April is the cruelest month, he told his wife. She asked him where he got that, and then she asked him why. Because it's starting to get nicer, he said. So if it's getting nicer, why do they kill themselves? his wife questioned with a typical lack of grace. Because everyone else is cheering up, and they are left alone feeling blue, said her husband. They figure out it is not the weather.

The tour group was to be fairly small. It's a little spendy, Keith informed his neighbor—as if he, Keith, had taken the initiative to research the trip and was willing to pass on information. I'm glad he's going, commented Keith's neighbor, who was kind. So am I, said Keith's neighbor's wife, who was not.

Keith's group was to join up with others in Zurich—a contingent from France or Germany—before continuing on to Africa. If it's Germans, Keith told his neighbor, they will speak English. Germans almost always do, they speak it better than you or me. If it's French, they probably won't speak English. The French act like everyone should speak French, said Keith, who had received all this information from his deceased wife Mary's sister Eileen, via phone.

Keith wondered if most of the French or Germans would have made previous trips to Kenya. He thought they probably would have, being closer. He hoped they weren't going to be full of themselves about it. Eileen, who had once joined a tour to the Holy Land, said they might well be. Keith didn't want the Germans always telling him what to expect, and he didn't want the French to make him feel as if nothing mattered, as Eileen hinted they might do. He wanted to see things for himself and try everything. He wanted to hear what the Kenyans had to say.

The RealRoutes gal provided Keith with some travel tips. They were listed on a mimeographed sheet titled Amazing Africa! The small "a" of Africa had teeth, representing the open mouth of a roaring lion. There was information about what to avoid. Tap water, fresh vegetables, false directions. Under Clothing, the sheet said to avoid synthetic fiber. Because of the heat and some business about breathing. When they got to talking, the gal gave Keith a catalog called Trek*Garb*, her own copy for him to borrow over the weekend. The cover had a photo of a laughing couple wearing baggy shorts and lace-up boots with rumpled socks. They were standing beside a jeep, holding maps and water bottles and squinting into the sun. The man had neatly-trimmed, silvery hair, and the woman wore a ponytail and had a sweater knotted around her neck. She appeared to be fairly young, or at least in good shape.

Keith looked at the catalog before dinner on a Friday night. He read about ponchos that had all seams sealed to be watertight. He read about vests that were relaxed yet roadworthy. He read about shirts that let perspiration escape while preventing rain from seeping through.

It had been a long week at his temporary office. It was either too hot or too cold in that place and the lighting was bad. This was to be his final office, most likely, since he was semi-retired. For the first time in his life, at age seventy, he was independent. On his own. Hanging out his shingle. Originally, Keith thought he'd have a small room at the end of the main hallway of the offices of Blackwood, Cates, and Cheff, the law firm with the rental space that had become available while the firm was between interns. But there had been a fire and the entire building had to be gutted because of smoke damage.

The building used to be a mortuary and crematorium before it was converted into law offices. Prior to that it had been a family home, one of the first families of the town. The recent fire had started in an adjacent apartment building where many elderly eccentrics lived. Both buildings were in an historic, rundown neighborhood that was just starting its rejuvenation program, a phrase the Downtown Collaborative liked to use in its many grant applications.

The planned renovation did not represent much of a financial setback for the firm, only inconvenience. The offices had been due for an update. The new space would have halogen lighting, sconces, sky-lights, a full, remodeled kitchen for coffee breaks or caterers, granite countertops, textured walls, and hardwood floors. But for now trailer houses had to be used, or modular units, as the contractor called them. These were set up in the circular drive and on the street. Then the builders went to work.

The only people with the law firm who regularly were present at the modular units were the receptionists and secretaries. The partners popped in only occasionally. Because of the remodel, they mostly worked out of their dens at home. Keith's home didn't have a den. There was no suitable place there for clients. He didn't suppose the lawyers entertained clients in their dens at home either. He didn't know how they arranged to see them—certainly not at the modular units, where clients would have to go tripping over two-by-fours and rolls of linoleum and stacks of tile to reach their appointments. Maybe the lawyers faxed everything. Maybe they telecommunicated. Keith had signed up for some training sessions on telecommunication, but he quit when he realized how embarrassing it would be to confess he didn't even use email. His old office space had access to a copier, that was it for technology. When he left, it stayed put.

Maybe the lawyers were all on vacation.

Keith hung a temporary sign next to his modular door. Keith Carson Insurance, green letters against white. He figured he'd be in full retirement by the time the new offices were ready, but he couldn't face trying to find new digs at this point, and there was nothing much that fit the semi-retired budget anyway.

Keith knew the youngest partner, Stan Blackwood, from Rotary Club, that's how this all had worked out. He'd known Stan's dad from way back when. He and Stan's dad used to steal chickens together to use in fraternity initiation rituals. They'd butcher the chickens and drain the blood into a jam jar. He told Stan about it. Stan didn't laugh or seem particularly amazed. He'd always been a solemn little fellow. His grownup self just stood there in line at the Rotary luncheon, holding his plate, waiting for a signal that would confirm the story was over.

Keith had been raised to laugh even if a story wasn't funny. To say, "Is that so!" or "I'll be darned!" even if a story wasn't amazing. To do this in order to be kind. He'd raised his own son to be that way, and he *had* been that way, even when he was down, he used to say, "No kidding!" just to be kind. But most of this younger crew didn't care about that. They didn't not care, they just didn't really think about it. "Kind" simply wasn't something they strove to be. It had no motivational cachet, Keith guessed, remembering that expression from some investment seminar. No clout. No punch, whatsoever. (The actual word "power" was rarely used these days, but that's all these little fellas were about.)

Stan's dad had been a kind man. A kind, kind man. He'd been that way in college and he had stayed that way right up to the end. Extra kind. The real thing. He'd given Keith's son a job there at the bank, when Keith's son had been having trouble, no questions asked. When the job didn't work out, he told Keith in private that Keith's son was a fine young fellow, a true human being, the genuine article, and he knew that he'd soon get his feet on the ground.

Stan's dad would have been devastated, heartbroken—wrecked! —to hear of the accident. Keith's wife Mary would have been all those things, too, and more, but she had been dead for so many years that Keith no longer shared in her imagined responses. Mary was plain gone. Stan's dad had been dead for only a few years, and he was still around for Keith, less and less each day, true, but still around a little bit, still in the air. "Wrecked!" he'd have said. It was the very least Keith expected from people. But, when it came to his son's accident, it was a condition no one alive seemed to be experiencing, not counting himself.

Certainly Stan, his good friend's bland little son, was not wrecked by news of the accident, the awful fact of it, even though he and Keith's son had gone through St. Catherine's together and graduated the same year from high school. Stan never even made those oblique hemming and hawing noises that are sometimes used by men to signify or acknowledge sorrow. At the funeral Mass, standing up front with the other pallbearers, he had looked at his watch. From across the aisle, standing in the front pew with Mary's sister Eileen and her daughter and the baby, Keith *saw* Stan do this. He had looked at his watch. At the cemetery Stan had walked a few yards from the waiting grave and made a quick call on his cell phone, turning away discretely, but not before Keith saw the glint of silver in his palm. At the luncheon provided by the church guild, Stan had piled his plate high with ham slices and cheesy potatoes and Jell-O salad with marshmallows, just as he had done at the luncheon after his own father's funeral.

Keith guessed that Stan, whatever else he might feel, saw these gatherings, these sad funerals, as well as the Rotary luncheons and the various Downtown Collaborative shindigs, as opportunities to eat a lot of stuff he normally wouldn't. Keith guessed this because once at a Downtown Collaborative fundraiser he had been trapped in a fairly long conversation with Stan's glowing, pregnant wife about fibrous root vegetables.

For many weeks after the funeral of his son, his only beloved son—with its Jell-O salad aftermath, so difficult to get through, even though the church guild gals meant well, staring at him (as they stared at all recently bereaved) with big owl eyes from behind their glasses, adjusting their expressions to convey bland compassion instead of intense interest—for many weeks that after a while became months, Keith walked the streets right in public, going to work, going to Safeway, sometimes going to Rotary on Wednesdays, with a huge, gaping wound in his side, as if he'd been opened up and left that way, and with a vice grip around his chest. He took ragged gulps of breath while watching TV, loud inhalations that made the house pets sit up and take notice, his body's way of crying, the doctor at Now Care told him, because he was too shocked by grief to make tears, because his tear ducts—the young doctor at Now Care told him, with little apparent care at all—were malfunctioning.

And after those many weeks, then months—months during which Keith's son was inside Keith's heart and brain and all of his organs, even in his veins and arteries, and they both, mixed together like that, Keith and his son, walked the streets and watched TV and went to the doctor at Now Care with malfunctioning tear ducts and chest pains and breathing problems—after all this time, which was really no time at all, which was really just the very beginning of the end of his life, Keith one day woke up. He woke up in the morning feeling semi-okay. He woke up feeling rejuvenated, just a bit, partially restored for no particular reason other than the fact that he was still alive. *Still alive.* He felt better. The pain, though, had been replaced by a thick, clammy residue of guilt that would take another long while to go away. His son, Keith woke up to discover, had left Keith's body. And he felt at fault. *Through my fault.* His son was alone somewhere, *through my fault,* he was in the water, *through my most grievous fault,* he was in the air. Keith's son was alone, and he was leaving the world, floating away, higher and higher.

That day, the day he woke up feeling better, Keith, unexpectedly even to himself, launched into his chicken blood story at the weekly Rotary luncheon. The chicken blood story was one of Keith's favorite stories to tell. It used to make Stan's dad weak with helpless laughter. It was a story that made his own son, his beautiful son, who was as kind as he could be, at least say "No way!" or maybe "Get out of here!" But when Keith gathered himself together at the Rotary luncheon that day and told the story to Stan as they both waited in line for the salad bar, Stan didn't laugh and he didn't exclaim and he didn't ask what the blood was *for,* which people might do, which then would have led to a *really* funny story. Stan just asked, after a blank silence, his small, clean fingers clutching his plate—"What did you do with the chicken?"

Christ! Keith couldn't remember what the hell they'd done with the chicken. There was enough blood obtained to anoint the pledges (he would have enjoyed telling Stan how) and that was that. He didn't remember anything about the chicken, post-slaughter. And Stan's dad wasn't around to ask. Or anyone else who had participated, it seemed.

They didn't cook and eat the chicken, he did know that. They should have, he supposed. He knew they probably should have.

A Kenyan came to speak at Rotary not too long after that, a visiting professor from over at the university. Keith had thought the Kenyan might talk about chicken sacrifices. He remembered seeing something along those lines in a documentary on PBS called *Africa,* just that, though it was a series covering the whole nine yards, the religion, the way of life, and so forth. (And yes, they did it like the fraternity boys, the chicken killing business, only then they ate it, sure enough, to complete the ritual, the narrator said, something about transformational process, spiritual alignment... Keith nodded off during the show.)

If Stan's son had been offended by the chicken blood story, for Christ knows whatever reasons, the Kenyan's talk at Rotary might have been a chance for Keith to ask some questions, show some seriousness. But the Kenyan's talk was about the ecology of tourism, at least that had been in the title. Keith didn't remember a whole lot about it. He did remember that the Kenyan wore a V-neck sweater and pressed slacks. And he remembered the follow-up discussion, all about apartheid, which seemed to make the Kenyan impatient. But a South African had come the year before and people still had questions.

~

Keith waited for his dinner to heat in the oven. He didn't think that Stan's son was especially offended by the chicken blood story. He just had no sense of humor. And he also had no manners. He had no *grace*.

The dog and the cat joined Keith in the kitchen while he looked through the RealRoutes gal's Trek*Garb* catalog. He read about pants that had an uncanny ability to shed wrinkles. He read about wicking underwear with moisture exchange technology. He read about amphibious sandals that said "summer".

Keith was accompanying his EatRite dinner (chicken Alfredo tonight) with a Johnnie Walker and soda, something he now only let himself do on Thursdays, Fridays, Saturdays, and Sundays. Pressing the catalog flat, he read about wide-brimmed, packable sun hats. He read about vented capes with sturdy mesh lining. He read about a bush jacket that was too urbane to be merely a wind shell. The straight bottom hem of this jacket, which was something like a shirt, could be tucked in or left out, to suit a more formal mood, or the moment's *joie de vivre*. On the opposite page there was a photo of giraffes in the distance, eating leaves from a tree.

Keith looked closely at the jacket. It had a lot of extras—flap pockets with Velcro fastenings, an optional belt, a secret ventilation system. The color shown was Sage, which was kind of greenish. The jacket wasn't worn by an actual person, but the arms were rumpled and the waist had a tuck, as if its phantom model had turned to inspect something on the horizon, the giraffes maybe.

Keith got the stubby pencil he kept by the phone and circled the item number. He pictured himself wearing the jacket. He wasn't keen on green, and he didn't think he'd want Savannah either, which was kind of yellowish. He'd probably go for Dusk, which was gray-blue. Or maybe Earth, brown. He pictured himself shrugging into the sleeves and snapping up the hammered nickel snaps.

Reaching to the top shelf of the cupboard, Keith fumbled around until he found a can of cling peaches in heavy syrup. He opened it with the electric can opener, the cat rubbing against his pant leg at the sound. He found a clean fork in the dishwasher and ate the peaches from the can, stabbing the slices two at a time, the fork shaking a little between bites. He had a hand tremor that tended to be more pronounced in the evenings. When he went to the young doctor at Now Care about it the doctor said, "You have a hand tremor."

Keith looked again at the jacket. It had 4 percent spandex for just the right amount of resilience. It was a little spendy, but he figured he could wear it year-round, in all kinds of weather, alone or under a coat, to all kinds of events.

He could wear it to a Lady Lynx game. People said the Lady Lynx played a better ball game than the regular Lynx. They had hustle and spunk. There was a lot of talk at Rotary about the players in the starting lineup, who reportedly had get up and go. Keith didn't really understand all the stats lingo, but he tried to show an interest. Somehow, he'd missed out on taking an interest in organized sports his whole life. He had liked individual sports in high school, the shot put, the long jump, that sort of thing. And after Mary died he had tried golf, going by himself because his game was slow. His son seemed to like these kinds of sports as well—at least, he'd sometimes jogged. You could just go out and do athletics of one kind or another back in his day, Keith remembered telling his son. You didn't necessarily have to *be* anything.

Keith had never even seen gals play college ball. He'd long ago learned not to highlight facts such as this, and he'd learned not to call them gals. There was often an update on the Lady Lynx's conference standing at the Rotary luncheon. All this season, his neighbor had been urging him to take in a game.

Keith looked at the clock. His TV programs would soon be starting. He poured his second drink, short this time, one measured shot and plenty of soda. Then he put the Johnnie Walker bottle back under the sink. He put the stubby phone pencil next to the phone and took a pen from his shirt pocket. He found the catalog page with the order form and peered through his glasses at TrekGarb's explanation of sizing. That gal (lady . . . woman . . .) that person from RealRoutes might appreciate the chicken blood story. Maybe there would be a good time to tell it. Maybe when he returned from Africa.

He flipped back to the page with the jacket and looked at it again. It was displayed in a companionable way next to the TrekGarb Genuine Article Cotton Weave Kind-to-the-Skin Travel Shirt (Extra Soft, Extra Cool, Extra Breathable). The shirt was button-up but had no collar, which struck Keith as rather youthful. It looked as if it were fluttering slightly, as if worn by a runner or blown by a breeze.

Keith filled out the order form, choosing Dusk. Then he crossed that out and switched to Earth. The dog watched him lovingly, and the cat pretended nothing mattered.

8.
Plague Pills

Something was in the air, there was a palpable lift in the mood of the tour, the disposition had switched from a guarded alertness to a free-wheeling *je ne sais quoi* as everyone tucked into the breakfast buffet—waffles, French toast, pancakes, bacon, sausage, ham, scrambled eggs, fried eggs, boiled eggs, papaya, pineapple, bananas, strawberries, muffins, bagels, croissants, Danishes, toast, yogurt, cereal, oatmeal, granola, orange juice, guava, mango, prune and pineapple juice, custom-made omelets, bloody beef prime rib, and all the Asian breakfast offerings, dishes involving tofu, eggs, steamed fish, dried fish, star fruit, seaweed, scallions, cucumbers, ginger, mango, rice, egg rolls, sticky rice, rice noodles, sweet rice balls, soy bean porridge, steamed dumplings, fried dumplings, soy sauce, lemon grass, papaya, chives, chili oil, sesame oil, and garlic-chili paste.

People were chattering happily about their rip-off experiences, near-disasters, and other untoward events of the day before. Alfred and Iris were certain that the clerk at the Fine Day gem store made multiple receipts for a small jade candy dish they'd bought as a gift for Iris's mother, an act Mr. Small proclaimed to be "wicked in the extreme."

"He took the card out of their sight to run it through the machine." Irene was the bearer of the news, since Alfred and Iris seemed disinclined to speak before any gathering of more than two.

Alfred was calling the 1-800 number that morning and canceling the card. Iris murmured this information to Irene, who passed it on.

Up until this moment Alfred and Iris had been noticeably tired and at sea, lagging at the tail of the group, worriedly examining their money, missing many of Ron's comments, Iris stopping periodically to adjust the laces on her Naturalizer Walkers, then scurrying to catch up with her husband. But their brush with fraudulence had given them a tinge of vigor. Wearing small, matching smiles, they listened as Irene conveyed to the group the gist of the incident. Luckily, they had a different card in reserve, Irene reported on their behalf, and they planned to keep a sharp eye out for similar behavior.

Pete said that a young boy sidled up to him as he stood in line at the bathrooms outside yesterday's temple and asked if he would be interested in procuring girls or drugs. Or he may have been asking Pete if he wanted to buy one of the temple rubbings that he carried in a small sack.

"He may have said 'temple rubbings,' or possibly 'temple rubs,'" Pete speculated, coughing loudly so that the elderly man with the bolo tie had to repeat his question.

"And what are temple rubbings?" the elderly man inquired with a certain delicacy, as if this might not be an appropriate breakfast table topic. Pete wasn't sure. It was a kind of art. Denise, who sat with her elbows on the table, forehead in her hands, fingers pushing her hair straight up, injected a short, snorting laugh into the old man's next response, which was something about "strange things...in their blood..."

Anyway—Pete continued—he thought that the boy might have said something about girls or drugs. When Pete tried to quiz the boy more closely he wandered off.

Keith reported that his pants were still breathing. This was a footnote to an ongoing group discussion about silk. Could you wash it? Throw it in a duffle? Was it as durable as the new microfibers? As cool? As cheap? The woman with the beaded bracelets experienced a bad silk situation right there in the hotel. A wrap was purchased from the hotel gift shop, proved to be wrinkle prone, did not respond to bathroom steaming, was returned. This was at some inconvenience to the beaded bracelet woman, who normally never darkened the doors of hotel gift shops, but the wrap had caught her eye as both attractive and potentially ethnic. Unfortunately, it had not lived up to her expectations, and, furthermore, it had disintegrated.

The woman was eyeing Irene with a bit of suspicious hostility. The previous day Irene had left the group after the morning's activity, which had been a viewing in a darkened room of a video about the manufacture of Fine Day jewelry. The Asian narrator spoke vaguely-British English, smoked a pipe, and wore a gemstone ring. He looked assistant professorial, or like a pop singer from the Seventies, rather pale, with hair over his collar. The narration hadn't quite matched the movement of his lips as the man invited everyone on a journey of discovery. Behind him, surf crashed. Then it was nighttime and village firelight glinted off faceted stones of various colors, rotating in close-up while village dancers perambulated in the shadows, doing intricate things with their hands. When the lights flickered back on in the Fine Day gem store viewing room, Irene, after some hesitation, left through a side door.

"I got in a cab," Irene said, when the woman with the beaded bracelets inquired. The Fine Day Gem Show had been an optional morning activity, after all. She knew she needn't feel defensive, but the inquiry was a tad aggressive.

"To go back to the hotel," she explained. "But we went around the city, just here and there." The braceleted woman quickly recounted a day in Nepal when she did exactly the same thing. The cab driver became her escort and she saw things rarely seen by the average tourist—an elephant carrying logs down a side street, a small shrine at a crossroads, children brushing their teeth right in a river..." and other incredible ruins."

Bolstered by her freelance touring (although it had ended up costing a lot more in cab fare than she had expected), Irene was eating from the Asian side of the buffet today and drinking hot green tea. She refrained from using the large linen napkins that lay like dentist drapes over the bosoms, laps, and knees of the rest of the group. She had a pleased feeling that she was managing to look rumpled and travel-seasoned in her cotton and linen clothing, as she listened to the other diners tell their tales.

The direst tale belonged to the man with the bullet bolo tie, who announced firmly that he had witnessed what may well have been a drowning. He saw it, or what may have been it, from his eleventh-floor window in the hotel. There were idling boats on the river, some with official-looking insignias. There was a long hook, a life float, people running along the bank. He couldn't see very clearly whatever it was that they fished out.

He was not offered very many encouraging comments from the group to go on. Some of them stared at him with no expression, as if waiting for the point or the punch line. But this was not a story of cultural quirks or devious tricks. This was not a traveler's tale, in particular. This was just death, which could happen anywhere.

Keith began busily rummaging through his bag, retrieving a small packet of antiseptic Handi-wipes. Irene carefully stepped around Pete's prosthesis as she made her way back to the breakfast buffet. The elderly man with the bolo tie waited a beat, his eyes alert and bright, then he began explaining to Denise the specifics of U.S. Coast Guard-approved flotation devices, segueing into a recitation of drowning statistics.

"Over four thousand each year," he said to Denise. "Over two thousand youths and again as many—or more—who are children under fifteen years old."

Keith rubbed his forehead vigorously with his Handi-wipe. Mrs. Small, who was perched with her plate in her lap, a fifth person at a table for four, began talking about methods of statistical analysis, saying "It needs to be emphasized that the method only yields statistically significant results if the number of data points is very large." Mrs. Small was a mathematician, Mr. Small explained. She waved a

sausage speared by her fork as she talked and looked as if she might
go on. Mr. Small interjected with a question about the day's schedule,
drawing Mrs. Small's attention to a time conflict in the itinerary.

Irene excused herself to use the bathroom. The tales of mishap
resumed. Keith reported that he started to get into a taxi-taxi last
evening, instead of into a taxi-meter, but he got right back out again.
This information came to the rest as a kind of tacit quiz, for Keith had
explained the difference in these terms several times over. He lapsed
into silence, then, his story over.

Mr. Small cleared his throat as if preparing to make an announce-
ment and then said that he was chagrined to relate that he and Mrs.
Small inadvertently sent Sterling off by himself in a cab. Sterling was
indeed a round-the-world teddy bear sponsored by a fourth-grade
classroom in the heartland. The Smalls were to be escorted by Sterling, or vice versa, for the duration of the tour, then they would pass
him along to some other traveler or travelers (the hand-off taking
place outside the environs of an airport, in keeping with airport regu-
lations), and his journey would continue. Dispatches en route would
be sent to the schoolchildren, as requested on a laminated instruction
card pinned inside the flap of Sterling's waistcoat, so that the class
could trace the bear's travels on a world map. The Smalls already had
sent to the school several postcards.

"The bear will go hither, thither, and yon," said Mr. Small.

"The bear will journey around the world capriciously," said Mrs.
Small. "Like a virus."

Sterling had been entrusted to the Smalls at the Starbucks in
SeaTac by an oral surgeon from Tampa. The woman with the bracelets
proposed that the oral surgeon hadn't actually escorted Sterling anywhere. She said probably someone gave Sterling to the oral surgeon
at his arrival gate, in direct violation of airport rules, and probably
Sterling accompanied him only as far as the Starbucks. The oral surgeon probably engaged in conversation with the Smalls as they waited
in line for their espresso drinks, simply so he could foist off the bear.

The elderly man with the bolo tie thought the whole business reeked of criminality. He thought the Smalls should shake Sterling down, check his clothing and press his belly, in case he was carrying contraband, or possibly a small, lightweight bomb. The Smalls laughed as if this were hilarious. It was true, they did not report to airport authorities the fact that they'd acquired Sterling inside the terminal, and from a stranger. But Sterling seemed just fine, they said. They were attached to him and did not find him suspicious.

The Smalls were preoccupied still by their previous days' misadventure. They told it in some detail, "to expunge it from memory," they said, in their quaintly loony manner, which was either charming or annoying, depending upon who was listening and the time of day.

After watching the Fine Day jewelry video, Mr. and Mrs. Small asked the store event host to call a cab. They, too, had their private plans. They weren't much interested in gems, Mr. Small told the event host. They were interested in handicrafts and folkloric items— embroidery, lacquerware, and the like. Their plans were to return to the hotel for a nap. The Smalls took a lot of naps, as the itinerary permitted. Morning naps, afternoon naps—they emerged with pink cheeks, laughing.

Ron frequently told everyone to take naps, whenever they felt the need.

"You will be so tired from your jet lag," he had assured them yet again yesterday, Day 04 of the tour. Then he urged them, in a brief moment that was atypically unprofessional, to consider him their Daddy.

"Papa Ron, you will call me," he laughed explosively into the microphone, just as the bus pulled up to the door of the Fine Day gem store, a stop not on the RealRoutes Chartered Quests PARADISE PROMISE—Amazing Asia! printed itinerary.

The Smalls' story continued. After defecting from the group (the event host did not call a cab, he merely stepped on the street and gave his head a jerk), they were deposited at the entrance to the hotel.

There was some subsequent confusion between the two of them as they fumbled for the fare. They were attempting to tip the appropriate amount. Keith had told them that a large tip "in this culture" (a favorite phrase) was insulting, and they had repeated this travel advice more than once to various others in the group, taking it to heart.

"Our money is a lot of money in their currency," the elderly man with the bolo tie repeated, with apparent reverence for the dollar's newfound status.

So the Smalls stood counting out coins in the local currency, making sure they did not exceed a certain percentage of the figure on the meter, Mr. Small employing a small, handheld calculator. The driver must have been impatient to get on with his job, for he jumped back behind the steering wheel after this transaction "with some alacrity."

Mr. Small indulged in a brief digression at this point on comparative work ethics and cross-cultural tipping practices, recounting an incident he and Mrs. Small had endured while on a trip to Belize that, if not for the exceptional performance of key personnel, could have resulted in an appalling misstep.

"Sterling," Mrs. Small said, and Mr. Small continued.

He and Mrs. S (as he liked to call her) were just entering the hotel lobby through the heavy glass doors (so nicely managed by the doorman in his green tuxedo), when they simultaneously realized that Sterling was missing.

"Sterling!" they both exclaimed, and the doorman stared.

They rushed back out and there was the taxi! Gone, then back, the exact same one! The driver must have made a U turn right there in front of the hotel, because there he was again under the protective archway, and there was Sterling, just sitting on the seat, perfectly nonplused, ready for another ride. The Smalls retrieved the bear and had a short conference then as to whether they should tip the driver a bit more, and after they came to agreement that yes, they certainly should, they looked—and the driver was gone.

There was a lull. The Smalls' story had not delivered the anticipated climax, and the momentum was lost. Keith was staring sadly at his itinerary, which quivered in his hands. Pete appeared to be taking a short nap right there at the table. Denise and Irene returned from the bathroom, where Denise had joined Irene as soon as the Smalls began talking about the bear.

The conversation turned to the food, how the eggs were rubbery today, how everything else from the breakfast buffet was marvelous as usual. The woman with the beaded bracelets looked through the English language newspaper, searching unsuccessfully for reports about incidents of drowning. There was quiet.

Then a gnomish little man who for some reason was sitting with them, even though he was a Unitarian, announced that his wife wasn't eating that morning because she was feeling unwell. A look of interest crossed the face of everyone within earshot. The woman with the beaded bracelets put down her paper. The elderly man with the bolo tie blinked rapidly, then turned his head to cough, dryly, into a cupped hand. Denise, lying prone now on the booth seat of one of the tables, raised her head.

"Unwell!" Mrs. Small repeated to Mr. Small, turning around to put her hand on his arm.

"Chills, achiness," the man said, his eyes sparkling with fellow feeling. "I believe she ate something at dinner that came back at her."

No one pressed him for details as to what exactly the phrase meant, but there was a resurgence of camaraderie among the listeners, some of whom raised their eyebrows to each other in knowing ways or patted their purses and pockets where stashes of Tums and Lomotil reportedly were kept. Mr. Small flashed a prescription bottle of antibiotics with an air of triumph.

Ron was spotted coming in through the heavy glass doors. They all finished breakfast and rose as one, ready for the day.

9.
(Re)visioning the Other, Aspects of
Mr. and Mrs. Small

They arrived during the worst storm in 100 years. The headlines were large on the front page of the *Honolulu Advertiser* the next morning. They arrived in the dark, after hours flying from Seattle, hours spent watching *Jaws* with no headphones (splashing water, frenzied panic) and Hawai'i Today—a promotional film clip with golfing, volcanoes, hula dancers, fruit displays at breakfast buffets, sumptuous desserts with whipped cream and nuts, and plenty of aloha spirit.

And then they listened to a wheat grower from Washington State talk on and on about his brother's experiences in the South Pacific during the war ("dubaya dubaya two"), and the vagaries of irrigation systems and cattle feeding, and the courses his son was taking at Pacific Lutheran University in Tacoma.

As the plane began to jump and drop and unexpectedly rise again, like an elevator gone berserk, all the flight attendants buckled themselves in—quite a squadron of them, for it was a big plane— even though the projected arrival time was over an hour away, even though no fatherly request from the pilot for them to attend to their safety in this manner had issued forth from the loudspeakers. Those passengers who could get a good view of the strapped-in flight attendants—perched on little jump seats, since the plane was full—examined their faces. The flight attendants looked serious. They would not make eye contact.

And then the passengers became very quiet and there was only the labored roaring of the plane and the lone voice of the wheat grower, a spare, gray-haired man who looked handsome and fit in a blue, polo shirt and a new Washington State Wheat Growers baseball cap. He sat with his legs crossed a bit formally and angled out into the aisle, as if he were visiting an aged aunt on a Sunday afternoon and couldn't quite get comfortable in the small furniture, his hands clasped conspicuously over a knee, his stiff new canvas shoes neatly laced. Up until this moment, the moment when all the passengers stayed put, seatbelts firmly clasped, the wheat grower had hastened to clear the path whenever anyone needed to get by, standing up and repositioning his cap to reveal a prominent forehead—pale white, compared to his weathered face and forearms, indicating that a cap was a daily fixture of his dress. Then he resumed his inconvenient pose.

The wheat grower's seatmates had gone mute as the shudders and swells became more frequent, but his own conversational impulse grew, almost in inverse proportion to their disinclination to talk. Possibly he didn't dare be quiet and make the human silence even deeper, as the plane shivered, and the overhead compartments banged, and unidentifiable crashes came from the service area. So he passed on—to all those people immediately adjacent and then gradually to a large portion of those in the coach class passenger section and even a few in first class, in a progressively louder voice that never lost its convivial quality—as much miscellaneous information as he could summon. He wracked his brain.

They learned:

His brother used to take showers on the island of Saipan with rain water collected in buckets and it was warm as it could be; his sister brought back a can of sorghum when she went visiting a sorority sister in Kentucky and said people ate it on grits, while he had thought only feed lot cattle ate sorghum; his son was getting all squared away again, after that damn 'Nam, in fact, he could do just about anything now he set his mind to; his brother-in-law broke four legs: motorcycle, tractor, horse, and cross-country skiing in the high Wallowas just the one time; he himself had a bum knee, which had kept him out of the service; his son could probably fly this plane, with everything he learned in that damn 'Nam; he himself had never been to Hawaii before, but his wife had; his niece should play basketball, what with her long legs; his brother had been a tail gunner on a B-29 in the fire-bombing of Tokyo; his wife might or might not go back to school; his wife had one degree already, in library science; his brother was buried in Arlington cemetery, and he went there to see the grave, just the one time; and his wife was waiting for him, right now, on Maui.

The man's voice continued, becoming ever more pleasant and ordinary, though very carrying, as the plane entered a situation that could be called dire. The passengers learned that the wheat grower's son's grades were up and down. They learned that this son had gone to Las Vegas over spring break and spent a night in jail. They learned that this son couldn't seem to follow traffic laws. They learned that he couldn't drive a car to save his life.

The big plane then ground its way downward to try to land. It performed a low, unsteady arc. It hung there in the air, seemingly immobile, as if it were trying to decide what to do. Mr. and Mrs. Small, who had been listening to the wheat grower's monologue and holding hands, could see white caps illuminated by the plane's lights, frothy specks in a jagged black sea, not so far below.

They weren't really Mr. and Mrs. Small. They were Henry and Sarah. They were married, but they were young. Barely twenty-five. They had their whole lives before them, as their respective parents in Massachusetts and Colorado liked to say, when referencing the trust funds. They sometimes called each other Mr. and Mrs. Small, as a joke. It was still a novelty.

The plane abruptly pulled up, away from the white caps. Its wings actually flapped, like a bird's. Unlike a bird's, the flapping was not intentional. It was caused by the 100 mph winds in this worst storm in 100 years.

Mrs. Small studied math. She already had two college degrees in applied math at this point in their shared life, and, after Mr. Small pursued his own educational interests on the island of Oahu, second largest in the Hawaiian island grouping (though no bigger than an atoll, or so it came to seem), her plans were to get a PhD.

The pilot, whose voice had been noticeably absent and missed by all, announced that the Honolulu airport was closed, that there were no lights on the runway, that the airport at Kona on the Big Island also was closed, that they would fly on over to Hilo. People slammed against each other as if on a tilt-a-whirl while the plane churned and bucked back up into the maelstrom, away from the perilous earth.

Mr. Small tried to think what country or general land formation was beyond Hilo. How much fuel did the plane have? How wide a swath did storms such as this cut through the south seas? How far did they go? Mr. Small wondered.

Later, when Mr. Small started his university courses and learned to say "King Kamehameha," and "Queen Lili'uokalani," and "Kapiolani Boulevard" without a hitch, he sometimes thought of that other really bad storm, the one that had happened 100 years ago. What had the people of Hawai'i been thinking as they heard the rain pounding the flowers flat, the *nanu*, the *okika*, and the *aloalo pupupu* (a kind of gardenia, a kind of orchid, and a kind of white hibiscus)? What had they been feeling, or dreaming, or worrying about when they heard the rain hammering on rooftops made either of tin or thatch? And later, what went through the mind of Queen Lili'uokalani when she heard rains and winds of once-in-a-lifetime proportions pummel the rooftops of 'Iolani Palace, where she was held a virtual prisoner for nine long months as greedy men carved up her beloved Hawai'i for themselves like it was a banana-coconut cream pie with nuts? What did Queen Lili'uokalani feel as she watched the Royal Palms through her upstairs window, saw them exposed in flashes of lightning, saw them toss their heads like crazy persons down in the courtyard, like hula dancers gone unseemly (a word missionaries might have used in the latter part of the nineteenth century), like hula dancers gone the Hawaiian word for berserk?

Did she feel a sense of impending doom, a foreshadowing of disaster? Or did she think to herself—This is it. It can't get this bad for another 100 years.

And just how screwed, exactly, had incoming traffic been way back *then* during inclement weather—the inter-island schooners and, earlier, the sailing ships of Captain Cook, with those optimistic names of *Discovery* and *Resolution*, and the Polynesian's outriggers and double canoes?

Mr. and Mrs. Small liked to say "screwed," and "oh fuck, oh dear," and "shit out of luck," etc., in situations such as this, during this particular time in their lives, when they were mainly Henry and Sarah. These terms, this specialized language, these coarse and disrespectful words and phrases ("rat's ass," for example), were inside jokes, very funny for the two of them, although they didn't know why. Maybe it was a separation from the mores of their parents, a liberation of some sort, a gesture toward possible ways of being. Mr. Small, especially, had most definitely *not* grown up with a potty mouth. But they never became particularly adept at swearing. Their private language of toughness and crassness gained its humor (they would have realized if they had thought about it) from the fact that it was in direct contrast not only to their individual upbringings, but also to the hesitant, modest tenderness with which Mr. and Mrs. Small treated one another, as well as the pensive, tremulous hope—perspicacious, nearly newborn—with which they faced the world.

Sometimes they would be sitting or standing, waiting for something, a bus maybe, or breakfast at the campus café and one of them would just barely touch the other's hand with a fingertip and then, not uncommonly, they each would feel flooded with a vision of his or her own childhood and the many steps they had taken to bring themselves here. At other times it was the future that flared up, a volcanic force of fate and destiny that filled them with awe. Sometimes both these things happened at once.

"C'est la fucking vie," they said, their eyes dreamy.

After Mr. Small began his graduate studies, the glow inevitably wore off, in part because of his newfound focus on kinship patterns, categorizations of ways of knowing, and the challenge of (re)visioning the concept of "place" in the face of internationalism (his tentative thesis topic), and in part because Mrs. Small had nothing to do in their crappy condo, and no cohorts nor colleagues, so was forced to watch TV. Nevertheless, they added new words to their swearing lexicon in an attempt to keep up the camaraderie, giving these words a nasty twist that was surely unprecedented.

"Up your diaspora!" they might say, feeling erudite and hip. "Fuck me indigenous!" Mrs. Small exclaimed once, in a fit of hilarity. But Mr. Small made her excise that addition, explaining that indigenous peoples here, as in most parts of the world, had indeed received such treatment, as Mrs. Small was well aware, and so this wasn't funny.

His lecture came during the cranky period, when the warming sunshine had become taken for granted, the daily dose of mango was making their bowels work overtime, Mr. Small had started to say "peoples" instead of "people," and Mrs. Small refused to go to the beach without Mr. Small, who wanted to study.

Despite a certain gregarious engagement with all the nuances of her environs, Mrs. Small was a creature of habit, Mr. Small decided. She was resistant to things new, reluctant to adjust. If an adjustment were effected, it then became part of what was slow to change, part of the habit she was a creature of.

"You could watch the surfers," Mr. Small offered. "Go on, ogle the Other!" He sought to maintain a sense of humor while also injecting a little sophistication into their shared discourse. He'd acquired a woven grass book bag, an umbrella made of oiled rice paper, and a serious demeanor. He gave her some ethnomusicology books to read, his special emphasis, but the books just sat there.

"Poop on your trajectory!" she said, when he invoked hermeneutics in his challenge of her assertion that his chosen discipline of cultural anthropology had a self-congratulatory tinge to it. Mr. Small would have liked to discuss Heidegger, Gadamer, Ricoeur. Instead, they argued about macadamia nuts. Were they as good as they were promoted to be? Did they taste like anything at all? Were they historically grown on the islands or introduced? They also argued about various practices to keep damp laundry from becoming mildewed in the closet.

~

One day, Mr. Small—in a concession to the needs of lay peoples, peoples who weren't currently graduate students, peoples such as Mrs. Small—suggested that they take a short trip to the Big Island, the largest island in the Hawaiian archipelago. They had driven around Oahu exactly once and had been shocked at how quickly the trip had been accomplished. They'd ended up eating their picnic lunch back at the Pacific Quest. This was an apartment building near Ala Moana Park and shopping center, a prominent landmark in the de facto *haole* gulag in and around Waikiki. Their studio condo, for which they'd signed a six-month lease, had generic American furniture with scratchy upholstery in Amish, quilt-like patterns, and secret societies of cockroaches that came out at night.

Mr. Small thought that it might help to visit somewhere larger. He also wanted to attend a cultural festival on the Big Island that his professors had mentioned. But he told Mrs. Small the trip was for a change of scene and to see lava tubes and sea turtles.

~

Mr. Small was enrolled in a class called The Sacred Art of the Hula, taught by a round-robin collection of teachers who all seemed preoccupied by other research. It wasn't a "how to" class, it was an "aspects of" class. The syllabus was a smorgasbord of topics. The students learned about various songs, chants, and movements (called "articulations" in the readings), verbal and nonverbal categories, and the system of *kapu*, or taboo. There were side lectures on acculturation and authenticity and otherness. They learned about *hapa-haoles* and whole *haoles*. Mr. Small suspected that some of the students who were enrolled in this class, random mainlanders like himself, very rarely, possibly never, saw actual hula, which seemed to be a private practice on the islands. They wrote papers with hedge-your-bet titles beginning with "An inquiry into..." or "Notes on..." or "A Survey of Theories About..." or, the most popular, "Aspects of...".

Even when they did see hula—when a film was shown, or a guest performer came to class or they were directed to the bars and lounges in Waikiki (even the Kodak Hula Show held transcultural significances, apparently, and self-identifiers)—Mr. Small somehow felt that he, at least, still had not seen hula, not really. He would deny he was hung up on notions of authenticity and the reification of the Other, that wasn't the problem, or so he'd claim. He just couldn't *see* it. Maybe because he spent so much time dreaming about it—hula performed in a warm, pattering rain, hula on the edge of a volcano, hula on the black sand by the sea. He felt that hula wasn't the Kodak Hula Show, not *really*. But he didn't really know what it was. His imagined articulations wove in and around the hula knowledge in his brain like smoke.

Mr. Small felt a strange, sorrowful longing as he sat in class taking notes, gazing out the window at the department's courtyard grove of bamboo, which looked so perfectly Hawaiian as it stirred and murmured in the breeze, but which, Mrs. Small had already told him, was not native.

~

"It is slowly sinking in isostatic adjustment to the great weight of the volcanoes."

That was the argument Mrs. Small gave for not going to the Big Island. Another reason was VOG. VOG referred to volcanic emissions, she informed him, which could have deleterious effects on one's health.

Mr. Small said that Mrs. Small really didn't want to go to the Big Island because she might enjoy it and she had made up her mind to resist Hawai'i and wouldn't be swayed. But Mr. Small also knew that Mrs. Small, even within their magical sphere of two, was, like himself, lonely. Finally, at his suggestion, she audited a botany class about the flora of the islands, and got a front office job in the math department (beneath her, but oh well), and the cranky period passed.

~

Twenty-three years later, even though they technically weren't elderly, Mr. and Mrs. Small enjoyed ElderTour, exploring new places and challenging ideas, mostly in Canada, the States, the Caribbean, and Mexico. On some occasions, Mr. Small might attend classes during these trips and had even, at Mrs. Small's urging, toyed with proposing that he teach one. *Old Frontiers, New Frontiers, Cultural Boundaries, Breaking the Boundaries, A Sense of Place, The End of a Sense of Place.*

(Note: Mr. Small failed to pursue academically whatever it was that had kept him so preoccupied in Hawai'i because he was kept plenty busy with Queen Lily's now, the tea shop his parents had financed on Seattle's Pioneer Square, while Mrs. Small occupied herself with an ongoing, several-decade math dissertation titled "Toward a Concept of Continuous Groups of Transformation Without the Assumption of the Differentiability of the Functions Defining the Group: Are Continuous Groups Automatically Differential Groups?")

To be in the company of traveling retirees made Mr. and Mrs. Small feel young, plus, it was possible to learn things on these trips. And there was no tension surrounding the question of meshing with the natives, for on ElderTour they were in a traveling classroom, respectfully contained within invisible walls. This PARADISE

PROMISE of Amazing Asia!, in comparison, was an unusual travel choice. They'd signed on at the last minute when "The Discovery Continues: Lewis and Clark Meet the Blackfeet" met with an undisclosed fate and was cancelled.

It was impractical to be traveling abroad at the holiday season, but Queen Lily's was well staffed and the prospect of six months without going anywhere was always dull. They liked being with each other in strange places, even if they argued. It made them feel like Henry and Sarah. Both traveling and arguing, they agreed, were enlivening. Happily, Sterling the traveling teddy bear had been presented to them at the airport, which gave an educational cast to the whole expedition, and provided them with a small source of sly, inside jokery.

"The bear is a powerful totem with many peoples," Mr. Small explained to various cab drivers, check-in ticket counter agents, and security clearance personnel.

"Totemism is characteristic of many primitives," he might add, patting the PARADISE PROMISE tin button stuck haphazardly on his Hawaiian shirt, in among the palms.

~

Mr. Small looked out the window of their hotel room on Day 05, beheld a pounding rain, and made a brief comment to Mrs. Small about that flight to Honolulu, so long ago, when they were mainly Henry and Sarah. Grabbing Mrs. Small around the waist as she proceeded to the shower, he said that it had been a true passage, a rough passage, one that could very well have found them lost at sea, one that could very well have marked the end of any ways of knowing whatsoever. Firmly positioning him at arm's length, with promises for a nap, Mrs. Small responded that the situation of the 100 mph winds during the 100-year storm had been nicely symmetrical.

"Unlike my nether regions!" exclaimed Mr. Small, giving her bottom a pat. Mr. Small had suffered testicular cancer early in their marriage, soon after they left Oahu, after only one academic year, and this had resulted in the removal of one testes. Not long after that, Mrs. Small discovered that she had breast cancer and underwent a single mastectomy with subsequent noxious treatments. It couldn't have been the VOG, they decided, since they never did go to the Big Island. It must have been the stress.

Since then, over two decades now, Mr. and Mrs. Small retained clean bills of health. And these events had not precluded the births of their three children—first Park, darling Park, named for Mr. Small's ancestor, the Mayflower one—and then—what a shock! –twin girls, Ali and Mona, names proposed by Mr. Small, as close to Hawaiian as seemed reasonable. The twins were just fourteen and driving them nuts. Thank God for Flordeliza, who drove them wherever they wanted to go in the Small's Saab, though she didn't look old enough to drive, hardly, or to be a nanny/au pair/mentor. (The Smalls could never settle on what to call Flordeliza.)

While the Smalls' bickering had not disappeared entirely, it did not express itself as especially threatening. Wealth, some earned, most inherited, made them comfortably tolerant, if not completely sane.

"Sharing new experiences is rewarding in every season of life" Mr. Small might remind Mrs. Small, as they emerged for the day, itineraries in hand, PARADISE PROMISE buttons affixed. (It was a wry shared acknowledgement that, in the touring department, they were somewhat slumming it.) The problem of cultural domination had remained on their marital radar, and, of course, it was a problem for the world in general. But their mutual lopsidedness, their literally asymmetrical conditions—they had long ago decided—made them equal.

~

Maybe once every five or ten years, maybe late at night, when a warm June rain beyond the open window reminded him of Queen Lili'uokalani, alone in her summer palace, Mr. Small thought of those days when he and Mrs. Small had lived in emergent love and tremulous hope on the island of Oahu. Or he might remember that time in Hawai'i while ordering teas from India, Sumatra, China, and all over, watching the occasional table of students relaxing after a tour of the Seattle Art Museum, students who reminded him of his own younger self, studying in the tea room of Honolulu's Bishop Museum, sifting through his notes from the lectures, trying to catch hold of something, be carried away.

Mr. Small had thought that if he could just manage to cast himself out into the world, far beyond the confines and expectations of Massachusetts, he automatically would have easy access to knowledge previously un-attained. But Mr. Small had found that he was mostly the same person in Hawai'i as in Massachusetts, that his propensity toward resolution was stronger than his urge toward discovery, and that—like the wheat grower from Washington State who beat back fear with miscellaneous information—his life now was full of details—pleasant, sad, ordinary, and strange—that served to diffuse and obscure the lacunae in his thought and the longing in his heart.

In other words, he never really did get a grip on verbal and nonverbal categories, indigenous expression, and ways of knowing. The concept of place had resisted (re)visioning. He passed that mission on to others. Sometimes he thought about these Others. He imagined them scattered all across the world—in a soft mist, on the edge of a volcano, in lecture halls and at podiums, on the black sand beaches by the sea . . . a great diaspora of inquiry, articulation, and yearning.

And sometimes he thought about that alien bamboo in the university courtyard, speaking softly to itself.

10.

The Skin You See

Denise snored. She didn't lightly burble the way some people might, the way Fred occasionally had. Denise roared with snoring. The lights went out, there were a few suspenseful moments, and then it began, an agonized blast of sound, mechanical more than human, animal-like, too, some cross between a jack hammer and a jaguar. It was a possessed sound with an anguished quality.

All night long for five nights Irene had been lobbing pillows at the head of her assigned roommate (the cost for a single was out of her budget) and whenever she connected the snoring stopped. But she was hesitant to actually shake Denise or roll her over, because she simply didn't know her. She didn't know her at all.

By Day 06 Irene was bleary-eyed around the breakfast buffet. She left Denise examining her elbows in the mirror of their large, marble bathroom, twisting this way and that. Irene hovered by the door, thinking she might say something about the snoring, inquire about it nicely, suggest antihistamines. Denise must be twenty years younger, at least. Irene could act motherly.

Denise twisted and turned before the mirrors, while Irene fussed with her new market shawl. Irene couldn't seem to make the shawl drape casually, as the woman with the beaded bracelets had taught her, a toss over one shoulder, the shrug of an adjustment. Theoretically, you just let it float there over your regular clothes—an intended, though casual, accessory. That was the only way not to look like a kid playing dress-up, or a crazy person, randomly wrapped, or an elderly patient trussed up by an impatient caregiver. Irene couldn't get the hang of it.

"I cannot fucking *believe* it," Denise finally said. "My elbows are crumpled. They look old."

She was still in her white cotton hotel bathrobe, which she liked to say was thirsty. Every time she put it on she'd say: "Now I'm going to put on my big, *thirsty* bathrobe." She had pushed her sleeve up and was pointing at her twisted arm held against her body, the skin bruised looking, like a spoiled peach, the elbow, with its rough folds, exposed to the mirrors.

"I have old elbows," she said, her squinting morning face going blank.

Irene looked away, embarrassed, and pretended to search for her key card. She didn't know what to say. Denise hadn't spoken to her that much, and she wanted to respond appropriately. She wasn't sure Denise was at all well. She had been sick one morning in the bathroom (and she wasn't quiet about it). And here she was worrying about her elbows, all the while sporting that hideous eye tattoo that her hair did not adequately cover, no matter what she might think. Surely it was temporary and a joke. Left over from Halloween, probably. It was quite rudimentary, just an oval with a beady little pupil and eyelashes like a cartoon. A Betty Boop eye. Certainly not like an "oracle," or however Denise had described it, whatever that was supposed to be. She said her friend Jimmy did it. Who Jimmy was, Irene didn't want to know.

Of course, temporary tattoos were all the vogue, or maybe not, maybe they only delighted the very young children, the cute little peanuts. Some of the women in Irene's First Wednesdays club gave them out at Halloween instead of candy. You could buy sheets of tattoos at the Osco in Crag, five sheets of fifty for $2.95, making the cost for each tattoo about one and a half cents. An alternative to turning out the porch light to avoid the highway robbery of trick-or-treating! But in the last few years the tattoos just made any child over five frown. Some put their tattoo back in the bowl.

Denise's elbows *did* look strangely old. Irene wondered how her own elbows would hold up to this sort of scrutiny. She suspected that they would hold up fairly well. Irene pumiced.

~

Irene noticed that Denise seemed to be preoccupied generally with her appearance. She disappeared into the bathroom with her makeup bag for long periods of time. Irene found this somewhat endearing, especially since Denise was rather unexceptional-looking—except, of course, for the tattoo, and the smudged black eyes, not to mention all that raggedy hair!—and she seemed quite invulnerable in every other regard.

Irene initially was daunted at the idea of sharing a room with this slack-jawed child who seemed to think that bib overalls and what appeared to be a swimsuit top were perfectly fine travel wear, and who did have that third eye staring at you, and the most unnaturally black bunch of crazy-cut hair. But the assignment was made, and Irene wanted to be gracious. When it became apparent that beauty was, after all, an issue, she felt more relaxed. Irene had sold *PAULA* cosmetics in the first years after Fred passed and could offer advice in that regard. She had a knack for cosmetics, as did her mother. It was in her blood.

At the end of a long day of touring, Irene liked to relax with a gin-and-tonic or two, never more. She had purchased a plastic bottle of Gordon's for this purpose—not at the airport duty-free shop (she was sensitive to the perceptions of others and hadn't wanted her newly-met traveling companions to see her heading for the booze), but back home in Arboleda at Wylie's Liquor. The Gordon's was the first item on her packing list, along with one liter of tonic, which made her checked luggage rather heavy. She also picked up a green plastic lime. Yes, she supposed they had limes all over the world, but who wanted to run around looking for them? And besides, she preferred the green plastic kind.

A gin-and-tonic was Irene's favorite alcoholic beverage. The word "tonic" sounded medicinal to her ears, prophylactic. Tonic had quinine, which would ward off malaria. Gin came from juniper berries, which had that sharp, clean aroma, almost like sage, so reminiscent of the northern plains. The taste of the two together, with a squirt of juice from the plastic lime, was like having a sour popsicle on a hot summer day on the edge of town, juniper and sage smells wafting in from the prairie.

This post-touring, pre-dinner, gin-and-tonic hour would be a good time for Denise to receive tips recalled from Irene's *PAULA* days. She could explain to Denise the idea of color points, the inverted "V." After her bathroom sessions Denise looked as if she had been irradiated, a comment Irene remembered her brother Herbert making, with regards to her own early make up attempts, when she was first learning the *PAULA* techniques.

She wished Denise would join her in a gin-and-tonic, but when she made the offer on Day 02, Denise took the drink into the bathroom. That wasn't what Irene had in mind. Irene would enjoy reminiscing about the parties, the *PAULA PAL* visits. These were occasions hosted by the customer. The customer would gather a few friends together and Irene would bring her *PAULA* products to the customer's house, along with the literature and price list. There would be something on hand for snacking. Before Irene began her presentation the hostess usually offered everyone a drink—a wine cooler, or what have you. Irene usually only sipped hers, having already had her gin-and-tonics. There might be three or four interested persons, or maybe a good-sized group. Irene would first tell a little bit about the background of *PAULA* products, interesting things such as how the softening techniques for the line of facial lotions had been developed by an actual hide tanner, many years ago. Also, how the first *PAULA PAL* parties got going, who *PAULA* was, that sort of thing. Then she'd do a basic makeover for everyone. The understanding was that the guests would buy some of the products, and they almost always did. Everyone knew everyone else in Arboleda; to not buy would have looked bad.

Only once was a *PAULA PAL* party less than a total success and that was when Irene's neighbor Tina hosted a party for her cousin Carla and her cousin Carla's friends visiting from Seattle, too many of them. The friends brought deli chicken from Safeway, and beer, and they laughed at the part about the hide tanner, saying they thought Irene had said "high tenor." When she finished the first makeover they all shrieked and said their friend looked like a drag queen. Irene drank some of the beer, to be sociable, even though beer always went straight to her head. It was all a bit much. She'd made her gin-and-tonics a little strong that day, nervous about the number of clients, and about the out-of-town perspective, and excited at the prospect of making a bit more than typical from product sales. But she was certain she was not slurring. She'd even practiced "Aluminum! Linoleum! Aluminum! Linoleum!" in front of the mirror before coming over, a tongue tingler that was part of her vocal training. Anyway, the friends laughed. And they bought nothing.

Irene would like to tell this story to Denise—edited, to highlight the rudeness—but Denise always disappeared directly into the bathroom at the end of the afternoon tour. Sometimes Irene could hear the shower running, and invariably the toilet flushing, but mostly it was silent in there except for the occasional slide and click of a lipstick tube and various squirting and spraying sounds emanating through the cracked door. Irene presumed that Denise was applying, or reapplying, her many lotions and makeup items. She'd brought quite an assortment of them, stuffed inside a polka-dot Quintessence bag. Surely, she must have some powder and concealer that Irene could help her apply.

At the gin-and-tonic hour on Day 07 Irene heard Denise shaking out her vitamins. She seemed very keen on these, also herbal remedies. Black cohosh was something Denise said she took for menstrual problems, mental troubles, some such thing. Irene inquired about this and a number of other herbs with even stranger names in various containers on the bathroom counter. Denise said her mother sold all this "health crap" through a private franchise, so she got it for free.

She looks as if she's been mauled by a bear. Irene snorted at her brother Herbert's imagined statement, then tried to cover up her snort with a yawn. She felt pleasantly relaxed as she gazed out the room's window at blinking radio towers across the river and jet trails vaporizing in the late afternoon sun. She thought about Denise's snoring. Antihistamines could help, and they were also good for migraines, allergies, daytime sleepiness, blood pressure, and cardiovascular this 'n that's. Or maybe that was the side effects. Or an aspirin and a hot water bottle. Irene let her mind drift. Black cohosh...Good heavens.

She sat up suddenly and smoothed her skirt. She had decided to engage Denise in conversation no matter what. She would ask her about Quintessence products. She would point out the effectiveness of concealer for blemishes, shadows, other anomalies. *Such as extra eyes!* Irene laughed with a gasping intake of breath, then cleared her throat repeatedly. She would mention pumicing. She could get into the *PAULA PAL* stories from there.

"You look nice!" She attempted cheeriness when Denise finally emerged from the bathroom after the usual stint of squirting, spraying, and shaking. Denise pulled a towel off her head and rubbed her damp hair. She had painted her stubby fingernails alternately violet and black. She didn't answer. Irene felt her face grow warm. She tried again.

"You have on your big, *thirsty* bathrobe!" An attempt to duplicate Denise's sardonic twist to the adjective. Denise stopped toweling and looked at Irene, her regular eyes laden with shadow and mascara, her tattoo bare and impassive. Her head seemed to be wobbling a bit, like a dashboard doll, a whatduhyacallit, a bobblehead. The eyes should be accented and highlighted, not gooped up. Irene looked at Denise's thigh where the bathrobe had parted. Denise was a wee bit pudgy around the upper thighs and midriff area. Irene noticed that she ate quite a lot at every meal, always going back for seconds and even thirds at the breakfast buffet. Irene wondered if Denise belonged to a gym or exercise group, something she herself had found to be a lifesaver.

There was another moment of silence. Then Denise spoke. "My skin is embattled by the environment." She said it without moving.

Irene laughed with delight, as if Denise had made a very witty remark. She crossed her legs and leaned forward convivially, hands clasped on her knee. More silence. Irene heard her laugh ringing, even though she had stopped. This was something she had noticed lately. She would say something to someone, make a polite comment, and then she would hear the exact words repeated in her head in a sort of instant playback. Same thing happened with laughs.

Denise began to comb her hair down to the end of her nose, peering through strands of it into a mirror next to the TV. Irene reached for her drink and took a sip, clicking the ice cubes. She put it down and freshened it, just a jot. As she opened her mouth to speak again—to say the words she at that moment was hearing in her head in a sneak preview that seemed to be related to the playback phenomenon—Denise preempted her.

"There was progressive loss," she said, her voice conversational. "But I've intervened early."

She turned to face Irene, blinking as if the sunset outside the window hurt her eyes. Irene stared, puzzled, her drink midway to her mouth. Not knowing what to say, she blurted out the replaying sentence that had been put on pause.

"Quintessence makes a nice product!"

"Excess oil. Surface oil. The T-zone." Denise seemed to be talking to herself now. "Skin can fluctuate wildly."

Irene swallowed and smiled brightly. Denise glanced at her sideways, as if assessing her ability to handle the idea of fluctuating skin.

Irene began to feel annoyed. It was so hard to make a conversation with Denise move forward. She shook open her Amazing Asia! itinerary and peered at it through her reading glasses. She reached over and freshened her drink, just a jot. She thought with a pang of her kitty Bisquick, who had to be put to sleep just before the trip, her defiant, tattered little body going suddenly limp. (Bisquick!) It was time, she had begun to yowl randomly and pull her stomach hair out in big clumps with her few remaining teeth.

"Where did Ron say we should meet to get our drink coupons for the Folk Arts Dinner Show?" Irene made her voice pleasantly neutral, the entire sentence replaying immediately in her mind. Then she downed her drink in one swallow and stood briskly, smoothing her fleece sweater with purpose.

"Underneath the skin I see is the skin I want." Denise explained, as if to someone else in the room, all of her eyes covered now by her hair, which she kept combing flat. Irene marched out of the room.

"Toodle-oo!" she called back through the door, striving for a jaunty tone.

Toodle-oo! Toodle-oo! Toodle-oo!... Irene's voice followed her to the elevator and all the way down.

II.

Foppery and Nonsense

"You will say Oh My Gawd!"

Ron was outlining for the group the plans for the day. He stood smiling before the breakfast tables, consulting a mental list and smacking the palm of his hand enthusiastically with his collapsed umbrella as he ticked off each item.

They were to see elephants carrying logs at the morning Native Life show at the Native Village Pavilion. They were to see a typical family of Villagers, going about their daily lives. They were to see ethnic costumes and ethnic dances, all authentic. They would be able to purchase folkloric items—embroidery, lacquerware, and the like.

And in the afternoon, the highlight: a really big Buddha. Ron did not elaborate. He knew, though, that they would be astonished. They were to be bused some miles from the Native Village Pavilion to see this Buddha. They would say Oh My Gawd. Then they would board a river launch and enjoy a dinner cruise home.

The elderly man with the bullet bolo tie remarked to Alfred and Iris that Ron invoked God's name not infrequently. Also, Jesus Christ. And there was a moment when he greeted them all at the breakfast buffet with "This is the day the Lord has made!" But when asked by the elderly man "What faith are you?" he said "Buddhist, Christian, Jew, many faiths. And Islam."

Keith seemed to have gained insider knowledge that this was to be a trek of some hours, no naps, no sneaking off in cabs. He was, accordingly, already clothed top to toe in versatile, any-weather travel wear. His shirt was lightweight, Keith explained, for the long haul, and there were mesh panels hidden under the arms. For a cooling breeze he could simply un...zip! a panel (after some fumbling the Velcro closure was found) and...(more fumbling) enjoy! It was a 60/40 blend. A blend of what? Keith was not entirely sure. Telephone wire and buffalo dung, Pete suggested to the Smalls, with whom he shared a table.

His trousers had zip-off legs. Keith persevered, staring pointedly at Pete. Then he reddened, at once aware of Pete's disability. There were several stories in circulation of how Pete might have lost his leg. One story was that it could have been Viet Nam, but Pete appeared too old for that, although he might just be unwell. Another story was that he had tried to unclog a lawnmower by kicking it. Pete had hinted at this.

There was a silence. Keith looked to Ron to fill it—maybe Ron had some tips about day-long travel needs. But Ron had sauntered off, his morning briefing over. He could be seen across the expanse of lobby carpet talking rapidly and pointing his umbrella at the chest of the doorman, who wore a broad grin.

Irene ventured a question.

"Is the shirt...cool?" Under her market shawl and over her linens she had on her fleece sweater. Everywhere they went was so air-conditioned. Here she was in a land of palm trees, always cold. She should have bought a stowaway jacket at SeaTac, one of those that tucked into its own pocket, a handy extra layer. Irene wrote that sentence on a postcard to her brother Melvin and Dad, back home. The postcard showed smiling Hill Tribe children crouching in tall grasses and wearing almost nothing.

"Yes, I believe so, cool," Keith said, as he directed his attention to his unfinished breakfast. He looked tired. Everyone focused on eating. Irene was having toast, orange juice, and coffee. The coffee, she said again, tasted like Seattle's Best. Morning was her most difficult time for making conversation. The orange juice she needed for the vitamin C. Because of her funny blood. No one asked her to elaborate.

Mr. and Mrs. Small were working their way around the breakfast buffet over the course of the week, choosing, in agreement, a completely different arrangement of items for their plates each morning. Today they were trying the same thing Denise was having—prime rib, the scalloped potatoes, and the corn pudding—a combo they reported to be a bit rich first thing. They asked Alfred and Iris what they were having.

"Oh...eggs," said Alfred, embarrassed.

"Yes, eggs," Iris confirmed, and she laughed a little, as if to keep the exchange going. It didn't. The Smalls were already talking politics with the boy who filled their water glasses.

"Yes, we have a king," said the boy, lowering his lashes and wiping the lip of his water pitcher carefully with a folded linen cloth.

"Fine, thank you," he added, apropos of nothing.

12.

Funny Blood
Irene

When Irene was seventeen she had her spleen taken out at St. Timothy's. This was before Arboleda had any kind of medical facility whatsoever, and you had to drive the forty miles to Crag. A splenectomy was prescribed for a condition called familial hereditary spherocytosis. Over the years she learned to give the long name a lilting rhythm.

Fa *mee* lial—hair *ray* ditty—suf *fear* o sigh *toe sis*.

It was mostly benign. Irene had no symptoms prior to her surgery, and there were no subsequent signs of this obscure problem. In fact, only when her sister Carleen began to get worn out, and then her other sister, Doreen, began to act anemic, was the shared "funny blood," as they came to call it, identified. Turns out they'd all had it for their whole lives. Some people got anemic or worn out, some people didn't. There was no way of telling. So a splenectomy was recommended, to dispel uncertainty. Plus, the spleen became enlarged, precluding careers in race car driving or stunt work in the movies or as a rodeo clown.

Carleen and Doreen were in college on America's Promise scholarships for disadvantaged rural youth when the funny blood was discovered—the doctors at the university medical center success-fully identified the problem when they both went in feeling dragged out and looking a little yellowish and peaked. Familial hereditary spherocytosis was just beginning to be thought of as a condition one could have. The university doctors wanted to study it, so they offered a package deal for Irene's whole family to come out there to Seattle from eastern Montana and get blood tests with radioactive tracers. Those family members who turned out to have funny blood would get a cut-rate price on their splenectomies. But Irene's family didn't go for the offer, opting instead to have their surgeries done by Dr. O'Neill at St. Tim's.

The blood got clogged up in the spleen somehow because either the white or the red cells were shaped all wrong. That was Irene's understanding.

She liked to say "splenectomy." It sounded more purposeful, crafted, and precise than "got my spleen taken out." But when people inquired further, which they sometimes did, she had to admit that she didn't know what shape her blood cells were—how, exactly, her blood was funny. For some reason she had never bothered to find out.

Irene discovered that she didn't really like to hear about what was standard or normal. Some of her acquaintances in Arboleda were the same way, she noticed. Sciatica made for fine luncheon conversation. Muscle tone did not. The exact specifics of the human body were not as interesting as the terminology of conditions. Scoliosis was a favorite, somebody's relative had it. A heart murmur was intriguing. Or irritable bowel.

"My cranky you-know-what," someone might say, to explain why they were late. Heads nodded all around.

People had been known to look at Irene doubtfully when she said that she was okay. Ever since AIDS, in fact, Irene downplayed the whole funny blood business. She sensed that familial hereditary spherocytosis, having had its day in the sun, had moved into the background of medical concerns. It had joined the standard canon of medical knowledge and was just another possible condition for being alive, part of the general overall description of humanity. What once was thought to be exotic turned out to be regular. Or just an anomaly.

It was being spleenless, now, that seemed to be regarded as a possible problem, and therefore a potential point of interest. Being spleenless was a topic that was likely to come up on First Wednesdays, the appointed calendar date for Irene and other women from St. Gerald's to gather for lunch at the Peak Café, which was uptown on the bluff, a gradual, two-hundred-foot rise from the prairie floor, the only elevation for miles. And if Irene had to go to Quick Care in Crag for anything, if her regular doctor was on vacation and she couldn't shake a cold, for example, the Quick Care doctor would question her closely about her spleenless state, ignoring the cause of it, the familial hereditary spherocytosis. He'd ask her when she last had her pneumo-vac. She should have this shot every five years, every ten years, once in a lifetime—each doctor said something different. She always answered, "last year," just to keep it simple. Then she got the prescription for a new kind of antibiotic.

Sometimes Irene wondered if she and other members of her family might not someday be offered a group rate to become objects of study on how well they all were or were not functioning. Functioning without spleens, that is. She wondered if there would be another recommendation for the removal of another body part, perhaps as a way of compensating. She wondered if that new procedure would result then in a new condition, which might lead to more special medical attention.

Only occasionally did Irene find such a prospect disheartening. Those occasions might come on certain days in mid-March, when the advent of spring felt uncertain and Lent was going on too darn long, when the wind blew top soil from the fields of the surrounding, bone-dry farms all across the town, and the only colors in the world seemed to come in cotton/poly knit, colors that occurred nowhere in nature, or maybe it had been such a long time since summer that everyone had forgotten. On those days, Irene felt fairly old and somewhat vulnerable, progressing, inexorably, toward an eventual death.

But most of the time Irene's atypical health history made her feel equipped with pertinent facts, marked with a special condition that was appropriately "managed." She watched the evening news at the cocktail hour and pictured herself as one of those interesting mature women in the commercials for One-A-Day Women's with Extra Calcium, walking around their yards or gardens with watering cans. Reasonably pulled together, full of hope. Attractive, strikingly attractive! A rose, rare and exotic, a little-known species, yes, someone with something about her, in possession of an unusual (yet competent!) charm.

Irene's long, white scar on her stomach was made in the days when surgery was not too delicate.

"You look like you were drawn and quartered and put back together again," said Irene's brother Melvin in the longest sentence ever to issue from his mouth. He said this at dinnertime once. It was a year or so after the surgery, and he'd seen her scar by accident earlier that day when, thinking she was home alone, Irene had dashed down the hallway to the bathroom in just her jeans and her bra. Melvin's unusual verbosity had been prompted by acute embarrassment. He uttered nothing at that moment in the hallway, of course; he just went back out to the tractor with his water jug, a rinsed-out gallon milk container filled at the tap. But then he must have worked all afternoon preparing his sentence.

It had been ages now since anyone other than herself had seen Irene's scar. She hadn't worn a two-piece bathing suit in years, and she didn't walk easily naked to the showers as some women did at the Arboleda Health Facility, which was built by the Skagit brothers two years ago when their Mongolian Bar-B-Que went belly up. She wouldn't sleep with men casually. She hadn't, in fact, slept with anyone except Doreen or Carleen before Fred. And she hadn't slept with anyone other than her kitty Bisquick since Fred passed on. And now

Bisquick had passed on. (Bisquick!) Fred had never actually gazed upon her stomach much, not that Irene could recall.

She experienced a feeling of sorrow—with equal parts astonishment and irritation—when Fred unexpectedly died less than a decade into their marriage. But Irene was beginning to be comfortable now with the fact that he had passed on young, though she was careful not to say this out loud. (Bereaved. Irene pictured a wreath of flowers and a crown of some sort, placed upon her head.) Nor did she care to go into the details of his ice fishing mishap—the breakthrough, the vehicle submerging, the official conclusion of death by drowning. She didn't choose to speculate on whether or not Fred possessed shit for brains, the unofficial conclusion of her brothers. It didn't really matter. The ice fishing death had become fact, something one could convey to newly-met persons in order to carry on a conversation. The details were what they were and always would be, amen. As Fred himself said, the one time she accompanied him on an ice fishing venture and they stood there silently staring at the freshly-drilled hole for many minutes that eventually turned into hours: "It doesn't get any different than this."

At First Wednesdays, Irene might say, "After Fred passed away..." Or she might say, "When Fred was alive..." reconfirming her status of being Fred-less. She might refer to the ice fishing mishap, too, if anyone inquired. But this rarely happened, because the faces at First Wednesdays were pretty much unchanging.

~

Carleen and Doreen also had long white scars. Like Irene, like Herbert. It was a family coat of arms. Their mother, Virginia Vivian (called "Viva" by everyone in Arboleda, Miles City, and points between), turned out to be the purveyor of the funny blood. She didn't get the scar, however, because she decided against having her spleen taken out, even though it was enlarged. She told them all to go on ahead, as if the multiple splenectomies were a group outing to the Buffalo Bill Museum in Cody.

Irene's father—christened Lachlan, but called "Dad" by Viva, and "Chink" by most Arboledians—did not have the long white scar, of course. Dad was a small, quiet man who all through Irene's childhood could be found at the kitchen table during the noon hour listening to the livestock report on the radio. He did not have the funny blood, and neither did Melvin, who, every day since he started walking upright, sat listening with Dad, both of them with their shirts buttoned way up to the neck no matter what the weather, long sleeves buttoned way down, their right arms securely anchored with mugs of Tang or coffee. As it turned out, the "familial" part of familial hereditary spherocytosis was not inclusive. Only some kids ever got it.

It wasn't surprising that Irene's brother Herbert acquired the long, white scar. Herbert had always been different from Melvin and Dad in every way. Viva called Melvin and Dad "those two," Irene and her sisters she called "you girls,"—subdivided into The Big Girls and Little Sister—Herbert she called "that one."

Herbert liked to sing. Neither Dad nor Melvin liked to sing. They didn't like to make sounds of any sort. For talking, they usually just said "Well, heck," and this had nothing to do with the livestock report. It may have had nothing to do with anything, but Irene sensed that it functioned as a signal of some sort. It might precede a scraping back of chairs and a rinsing out of mugs, which they then placed carefully in the dish rack before going back down to the barn.

The rest of them liked to sing. They sang "Zippety Doo Da!" going to town, Viva driving the Plymouth. They sang "Up, Up, and Away, in My Beautiful Balloon," relishing the falsetto. They sang "Off we go, into the wild, blue yonder!"—the Air Force song. They sang "Lucy in the Skyyy, with Diamonds" and "Here, There, and Everywhere," in harmony. They sang "Chain, Chain, Chain…Chain of Fools!"—Herbert's favorite.

At home, they sang the Skye Boat Song—"Speed bonnie boat, like a bird on the wing!" This was in honor of Angus, Dad's trapper-trader grandfather. Or sometimes they'd break into some impression of Indian singing: "Way ya hay, my one-eyed Ford!" That's all they could come up with. They'd heard it somewhere, maybe sung by those Cheyenne girls at football games, tough girls who liked to dance, laughing and singing, in tight circles in front of the concession stand so that no one could get around them to buy the concessions, the popcorn and Coke and hot dogs with mustard.

Dad's Grandpa Angus had been in love with a Northern Cheyenne woman. That's the story Viva told The Big Girls and Little Sister, her voice a confidential whisper, her head leaning forward over the breakfast table. The woman's surname was Many Kills, and Grandpa Angus called her "Maggie." How Viva got her information was for her to know and them to wonder. There was such a thing as the Historical Museum in Crag, they might have heard. Still, it wasn't in there. Some people just knew.

Grandpa Angus had to say goodbye to Maggie, obeying his parents' orders, and he marched off to marry Grandma Inez. But first—first!—Angus and Maggie had a baby together, which was Archibald, who Maggie called Porcupine and everyone else came to call Beeb, their own Grandpa Beeb. After Angus marched off to marry, he and Inez took the baby Beeb, little Porcupine, they took him from Maggie and raised him as their own, giving him that goofy name, Archibald. So Maggie lay down in the Yellowstone River in the chilly autumn and piled rocks onto her own body in the shallow edges. She lay flat, piled on rocks, closed her eyes, went to sleep, and died.

Beeb grew up and married Grandma Rose. And Grandpa Beeb and Grandma Rose had two boys, Uncle Herbie, who died at Bataan, and Dad, who married Viva. And Dad and Viva had Doreen, Carleen, Melvin, Irene, and Herbert.

"Carry the lad who's born to be king! Over the sea to Skye." Everyone stood around the piano, Doreen playing.

~

Doreen and Carleen went off to college in Seattle through the America Promise. Herbert moved to town, then to Spokane, then all over. Melvin helped Dad hold down the kitchen table. That left Irene.

After she graduated from high school, she was going to go to Seattle. She had the America Promise application all ready to go, but instead she did a semester at Crag Community College, CCC. Only one semester, then back to the ranch. She was still feeling wobbly from her splenectomy. Back to the ranch, helping Dad, helping Viva, Fred driving out once a week, they courted. They courted for five years, before Irene said okay and they got married. She didn't really know why. Well, she partly knew why. It was because she wanted to go see the Grand Canyon in Fred's uncle's pickup camper, which he'd offered on loan for the honeymoon. As it turned out, the camper deal fell through, and there they were: married. But she didn't mind. She was earning a little money giving voice lessons in town and taking a couple more classes at CCC, driving to Crag twice a week.

Irene was okay with that path in life, the going to town and marrying Fred, though she missed her Mom when she moved, she missed Viva. And two years into Irene being married, Viva suddenly died. She died of a heart attack, after first taking her ritual walk to the mail box out at the end of their road, and then making her afternoon glass of Tang with ice. She was just resting there in the recliner, drinking her Tang. Then she died.

Viva's spleen had nothing to do with her heart giving out, Dr. O'Neill told Dad. He didn't know what made it give out. Viva didn't smoke, and she didn't drink. No one in the family did those things (except Doreen, Carleen, Irene, and Herbert). Dad had worried about Viva's spleen, but Viva never gave it a second thought. It was Dad who said he guessed that any kid who had the funny blood should have the surgery, and that Viva should have it too. That was Dr. O'Neill's opinion, and Dad tended to believe whatever Dr. O'Neill said, perhaps because he rarely had occasion to hear him say anything.

Viva said "Oh, pooh!" when Dad said he guessed that she should have the surgery along with the kids, and she invented a medical fact about having a splenectomy in middle age. She said that it would interfere with a woman's "plumbing" at a very bad time. This quieted Dad immediately.

But Dr. O'Neill concurred with the doctors in Seattle that Viva's enlarged spleen might cause her some problems someday. There was a danger of rupture.

"If I get bucked off my horse!" said Viva. "If I roll my pickup truck!"

Viva never rode any of their horses, nor drove the pickup truck even once. She said she couldn't do those things because she was from the city, meaning Miles City. Viva had grown up in Zap, North Dakota, and nearby Beulah, and when she was eight, her family moved to Rugby, the Geographical Center of North America. Then they moved to Miles City when she was ten. Miles City was the Cow Capital of the World and home of the annual bucking horse sales. Nevertheless, Viva stuck with her disassociation from all ways Western and rural, entertaining teasing, but no debate. It was as if she were saying she couldn't eat meat on Fridays because she was Catholic. Not a matter of capability, nor inclination. Just a part of the special prohibitions of her kind.

Irene felt that if she had not married Fred and moved to town Viva would not have died. It was her fault. But she couldn't share this feeling with Doreen or Carleen without them telling her she was crazy. She couldn't share it with Dad or Melvin, who pretty much didn't talk. She couldn't share it with Herbert, who was gone. So she just kept quiet and mourned. And time passed. And she and Fred went on the Europe budget trip and saw the Mona Lisa. And she missed Viva, wherever she went or whatever she did, to the current day.

~

Viva went to the Clip 'n Curl once every two weeks. She wore City Lights lipstick every day and a special kind of nail polish called Supper Club Shine. Way out there on the windswept prairie, eighteen miles from town on the county road, she wore polyester pant suits, taking off the jacket and hanging it on a hanger before slipping an apron over her floral print blouse.

They all heard the stories of the courtship with Dad, the blind date with no talking, the potato salad spilled in the lap, Dad's trips to Miles City. But these stories didn't ring with the resigned inevitability of other parental courtship stories, nor with any strong sense of long ago. The potato salad incident could have happened yesterday.

Dad's ways and customs were, to Viva, ever new.

"He puts ketchup on scrambled eggs!" Viva would remark to the girls nearly every morning while clearing the breakfast dishes in her quilted satin robe, her hair wrapped in something she called a sleep snood, stretchy slipper-socks on her feet.

Viva somehow had been transported from Miles City to the ranch ("I decided to go with Dad...") and she never looked back. It wasn't, exactly, that she looked forward either. It was an occasion if she went southeast to Miles City, and she ventured north then west on US Hwy 2 only reluctantly and only once or twice a year, setting off with trepidation in the big boat of a car as if she were crossing the seven seas, going to Havre to visit her cousins and shop at the K-Mart, one or more kids for company in the car. Yet she always looked as if she were ready to travel, and, it's true, she did make occasional pilgrimages with the kids to Seattle to visit her brother, her only sibling.

Irene had no memories of her mother ever helping Dad doctor cows out in the corrals before Melvin was able, or bumping the Power Wagon over the dusty bunch grass looking for downed fences, the desultory job of Irene and her sisters. What Viva did toward the ranch effort was cook, with gusto. She cooked tuna noodle casserole, meatloaf and mashed potatoes, roast beef and gravy, pot roast with onions and carrots, stuffed roast chicken, corn on the cob, pork chops in cream of mushroom soup, pork 'n beans, cole slaw, peach cobbler, cinnamon rolls, and rhubarb cake, and she made iced tea from tea bags, adding fresh mint from the side of the house and plenty of sugar.

This fare was sometimes improvised upon, or an exotic dish might make an appearance—vanilla ice cream scooped onto fresh cantaloupe, Swiss steak and mushrooms, a canned salmon loaf with crushed Fritos on top (only once), pineapple crunch, strawberry pound cake topped with Cool Whip, from a recipe on a Jell-O box.

Viva also—right after the breakfast dishes were done, dressed in a big shirt and old denim pants with an elastic waistband—cleaned. She washed and waxed the kitchen floor, she vacuumed the house up and down, she polished the living room furniture with Old English, she smacked and plumped all the pillows in the family room, she changed beds, replaced light bulbs, emptied trash cans, sprayed the back porch with Raid and shut it up tight for fifteen minutes, swept away the resulting dusting of dead flies, put up a new No-Pest fly strip.

She scrubbed walls, Windex-ed windows (and also the framed photos of her children and the more venerable dead pets, and 4-H cows), and poured Clorox down the drains. Then she attacked the bathrooms, shutting herself up in there with Pine-Sol and flushing the toilets vigorously. Herbert said she was going to kill them with all that cleaning. That was when he was in high school and always reading, every sort of crazy thing.

After the cleaning Viva tended her indoor plants, her exotic varieties, roses and African violets and so forth, which resided on top of the television cabinet in the family room. She watered them and snipped off the dead leaves, dusted them, and sometimes even polished them with a little Crisco to make the leaves shine. There was an orchid of some sort that she tended with the vigilant concern Melvin would give a sick calf. She called her indoor flowers her kids, which Herbert said was weird.

"I gotta give the kids their breakfast," she'd say, measuring plant food into the plastic watering can.

Then there was a quiet half hour in the bedroom while Viva sat and did her hair and face at the ruffle-skirted dressing table. There was a mother-of-pearl, hard plastic makeup case that had satin lining and a little mirror built in under the lid. First, she pinned into place high on her head something called a wiglet, which was supposed to be incorporated into one's existing hair, but which Viva wore like a hat. Then she rubbed on Oil of Olay ("oil of old ladies" in Herbert's vernacular), put on her City Lights lipstick, and donned one of her pant suits. She had an extensive, if homogenous, collection—each a different solid pastel, generously cut for her big-boned frame, some pure polyester, some cotton/poly knit. A few minutes later she removed her jacket, hung it on its hanger, rolled up the sleeves of one of her numerous, yet similar, floral print blouses, and started lunch.

Every day except Sunday, Viva took her after-lunch walk to the mail box at the end of their road, re-attired in her full pant suit. The three blue heelers, Snap, Crackle, and Pop, went with her if they happened to be off duty, darting ahead in a group like dolphins, jumping in tandem over the ditch. But that was it for Viva participating directly in ranch life out of doors. She drove the Plymouth to town a lot on various errands—getting Dad and Melvin some of the purple disinfectant they liked to swab on every living thing, buying groceries, maybe making a special trip for Clearasil for Herbert or some hair care products for the girls, singing "Proud Mary" to herself, tapping the steering wheel, her fingernails aglow with the Supper Club Shine.

~

Herbert was never as relaxed about his spleenless state as Irene. He didn't seem to find that it made him feel special, with potential spots of interest. Irene never knew what Doreen and Carleen were thinking, since they both had moved away. She regretted that she didn't know. She used to visit with them on the phone almost every week, back when they were starting their careers in Crag. And when Irene was first living in Arboleda with Fred, she talked on the phone with Viva almost every day.

"Love ya." They always ended their conversations that way. Even if they got into a big brouhaha about the wisdom of buying furniture sets on time, or about the unusual nature of Herbert's career choices (such as they were), or about who would cook what for Thanksgiving. After any kind of argument whatsoever, they always closed calmly and matter-of-factly with that comforting tag line.

"Love ya."

Losing Viva was nothing like losing Fred or losing Bisquick. Losing Fred was like losing a job, a situation. Losing Bisquick was like losing a favorite purse, only worse. Losing Viva was like standing there with your mouth open. Losing Viva was like having the wind knocked out of you, losing your breath, or the end of a sentence, standing there clenched with uncertainty, losing your whole train of thought.

It was her fault. It just was.

Doreen and Carleen hadn't mentioned their missing spleens in a long time, not that Irene could remember. Herbert was another story. He used to always call up Irene and talk about "compromised immune systems" and ask her if she'd had her pneumo-vac. He'd be full of stories about HIV or what have you, tainted transfusions, hepatitis C (the sex kind!). A lot of fun. He read too much. That's what she'd say to him. You read too much! He was always calling her up, night and day. He called her from Crag, from Spokane, from Seattle. Then the calling stopped.

Herbert, Herbert, Herbert. That's what she said at First Wednesdays, now, if anyone asked. Herbert, Herbert. The kid was a lot of fun. He read too much. Not such a kid anymore. Well heavens, neither was she.

Viva used to worry about him. Only Irene knew that. She worried about him when he played junior high football, she worried when he quit. She worried about him when he wouldn't ask anyone to the Senior Prom, she worried about him when he finally did and got turned down. Melvin's path in life, in comparison, was charted.

He had one high school girlfriend, Susan. They started dating in tenth grade and, thirty-odd years later, they were dating still. Melvin grew up with one desire—ranching. (Or two, farming and ranching, depending on whether growing hay was considered to be farming or ranching, a debate of utmost interest to Dad and Melvin and of profound tedium to everyone else in the family.)

While The Big Girls were away at college and "those two" were down at the machine shed fixing the baler, Irene, Herbert, and Viva sat in the family room, talking. Viva's conversation revolved around the gossip of the town, who made the cheer squad, who made a fool of himself at the Fun Days picnic. Or she made oblique speculations about the girls' love lives or wry observations about Melvin and Dad. She didn't know what to say when Herbert expressed worry about his funny blood and then about his spleen. Viva really didn't have the words to calm fear.

She didn't say "The universe is an ocean and we are merely flecks of foam on the crest of a wave." And neither did she say "Life is a river and the water of the river today will not be the same as the water of tomorrow, yet the river remains." Nor did she say "The paper reeds by the brook shall be withered and faded away."

She just said "We'll all be dead in a hundred years." This was as close to philosophy as Viva got.

"Everybody's got something." That's what she said to Herbert when he first heard about the funny blood and was dismayed at the idea that all along, unaware, he'd been different. Viva shredded the Kleenex she kept tucked up her sleeve whenever this topic came up. Herbert didn't notice this, but Irene did. She felt guilty, Viva once admitted to Irene. The problem came through her. The funny blood. It was her fault. She said that in a lowered voice over the breakfast table, only once.

"You might as well be this way as the way you were," Viva would offer, when Herbert started to get worried about whether spleens might not, after all, be necessary. Then she'd shred that Kleenex.

~

After Herbert took off to go here, there, and everywhere, he at first called the ranch almost weekly. If he happened to get Dad, he asked him a lot of yes-or-no questions. Was the baler working? Was that bonehead gelding getting half broke? He knew Dad's language. Was it still drier than a popcorn fart? Dad didn't like expressions of this nature, but was glad to respond to Herbert's questions.

For Viva, Herbert only had problems. His landlord was a jerk. He couldn't get used to the goddamn rain. Life was weird. Herbert always had been a whiner. Irene told him she thought that it was unfair that he saved his whining up for Viva, and that he seemed to want more from Viva than he ever got from Dad. So when Irene moved to town he switched to calling her, and she certainly got an earful.

Close to when Herbert stopped calling, cold turkey, he once got Irene on the phone and told her that he thought their mother was heartless. Something's missing there, he said to Irene. She's not in the real world. He even used the word "simple-minded." Irene hadn't known what to say at the time. When Viva died, Irene thought she might take Herbert aside after the funeral was over and give him a talking to. But she couldn't, because he wasn't there. They couldn't track him down. Here he'd been calling all the time and complaining about this and that, but, turns out, no one really knew where he was calling from. He never said anything real specific about himself, his workplace and so forth. And always moving, so by the time you called him back there was no such person. And then he didn't call and didn't call and didn't call. And the years went by, and he didn't call.

~

She would never forget it, lying in her hospital bed in a delicious haze, Doreen and Carleen laid out in beds next to hers, Herbert across the hall. They were in the children's ward, even though they were hulking teenagers, seventeen, eighteen, nineteen, and darn near twenty. She guessed the nuns wanted to cluster them, since they were anomalous yet related, and that's where the beds had been. These were nice nuns, like in *The Sound of Music*. They referred to Irene and siblings as "blessed children," or sometimes just The Blessed. There didn't seem to be anyone else in the children's ward. It was summertime and all the other children in eastern Montana were well.

The children's ward had boxes of popsicles in a little refrigerator down the hall—lemon-lime, orange, root beer, banana, and cherry. The nuns would bring the popsicles to The Blessed whenever they asked. They asked a lot, syncing the popsicles up with their morphine shots, which came often, in big horse syringes, it seemed, as those were the medieval days of hospital care.

They stayed a full week. Irene could hardly walk when it was time to leave, she was so used to lying in her bed by the window, trying not to laugh at the TV, wondering about her long incision and the stitches somewhere down there under the mound of bandages, eating popsicles, having morphine.

It had been scary, the night before the surgeries, which were performed all in one day, assembly line. And it was scary, having a big incision and knowing that only tiny stitches were keeping your guts from falling out. And it hurt, it was no small thing, being slit stem to stern!

But Irene loved to think of that time in the hospital, all of them together, she just seventeen. Carleen and Doreen back from the coast, each of them in her very own bed (adjustable!), Herbert across the hall. Melvin and Dad visiting every day at dinner time, caps in hand. All those hours lying next to her sisters (and Herbert across the hall), nobody going anywhere, nobody making plans or wondering what to do. Dr. O'Neill making his rounds and nodding his head and rumbling his approval as he checked her incision, as if she had done something special.

She loved her own little bed, right next to the window, which could be opened, since this was in the old St. Tim's. She remembered that it rained one day! What a blessed event in July out there on the flats! Her lips were sticky with popsicle juice, her body was cool and clean, having just been sponge-bathed and wrapped in fresh sheets, and she was floating, floating, floating... and the pain was going, going, going... up, up, and away... receding... gone.

The rain blew into the room in gusts, falling softly on her face, smelling of juniper, smelling of sage, and she was safe... and so cozy... with Doreen and Carleen, and Herbert just across the hall, having his own popsicle and morphine.

And as Irene closed her eyes, and opened them, and closed them... and opened them... as she drifted up, up, and away... she saw her mother's face. She saw the face of Viva.

Viva's hair needed freshening. Her wiglet was on crooked. So was her lipstick. Even through the beatific blur, Irene noticed that.

Viva came hurrying across the room to close the window, her expression (shot through with radiance, in Irene's vision) stern and detached. She tried to plump up some pillows, but The Big Girls groaned. She organized the things on the revolving tray tables next to the hospital beds, rearranging the ice water and lotion and magazines into arbitrary groupings. Then she resumed her nervous post in the corner chair near Little Sister, near Irene. Surrounded by shredded Kleenex, Viva jumped up whenever a nun entered the room and hurried across the hall to see Herbert.

Irene knew that Viva did not want assessments or prognoses or any information at all about this invisible condition. She was determined to concentrate only on the very next thing that she should do. *There is nothing to be done, nothing to be done...* We'll all be dead in a hundred years. Viva's philosophy was Irene's last waking thought, as the wind and rain arose in a gust and shook the pane.

13.

Weird Birds in a New Hotel

Everyone wanted to see the real city, provided there were no bed bugs, thin walls, illicit activities, people sleeping in the corridors, bathrooms out back, junkies, whoremongers, cheerless, lonely males, people traffic from the disco bars, or hookers renting long-term rooms for short-term use.

Irene sat at an umbrella table on the fifth-floor pool terrace preparing for the day's activities by reading her guidebook, *Go Now! – Asia*. She gazed at a glass skyscraper across the steely gray waters of the river. The building's body was segmented, like a giant blade of bamboo, and its roofline was angular, like a machete-d slice of sugar cane. Along with the Riverview, it was one of the newest buildings out on the edge of the city. A beacon blinked from the highest point. It would soon be lost in the dawn. Watching the sky change, Irene waited for the world to wake up. Her only companion was a smocked hotel worker who quietly strained bugs from the surface of the pool. He worked methodically and without expression, the long-handled net giving him the appearance of a stationary gondolier.

She had left her room in the wee hours, unable to sleep, and sat in the silent lobby of the hotel until she discovered that the pool area was open. Back in the room Denise's snoring was droning on and on. Before bedtime Denise had been rude, or so Irene felt. Irene had inquired about Denise's life goals, just generally, what was her job, what were her career plans? Denise said her plans were to be the first teacher in space. Oh, was she studying to be a schoolteacher then? Irene had asked with interest. No, Denise answered. End of conversation.

Irene looked at a paperback book she had picked up at the English language bookstore near the hotel the previous day. She'd grabbed it in a hurry, the bus had been waiting. *Enjoy Your Stay*. She'd thought it was a travel publication, the cover showed a black limousine in front of glowing, arched windows. Now, in the dawn's early light, she saw the fine print: English for Tourism and Hospitality Industries.

If go/butterfly forest/return by bus?

The instruction began with a section on the conditional.

Have/catamaran cruise/if go/Santorini?

This hotel, she supposed, could be anywhere. She imagined there were other hotels more authentic, more locally colorful. Maybe in the heart of the city. Would they have torn curtains, dim sheets, and crusty baths? Her guidebook seemed to revel in squalor. Of course, one would want to give a wide berth to things described as decaying, forgettable, boxy, or sleazy, and avoid anything that inspired use of the word "blight." But was it necessary to have helicopter service to and from the airport? (Apparently possible at the fanciest hotels.) Was it necessary to hear string quartets on the mezzanine?

An undeveloped scrub area shared the river shore with the hotel, an open moonscape of broken concrete and litter, far out beyond the poolside bougainvillea. A collage of cardboard, battered sheet metal, and shreds of blankets flanked a thin stream of sludge meandering toward the main waterway. A bulldozer jerked in the vicinity of these haphazard shacks, preparing the ground for new development. The sound of its engine—surely a rude blast for the shanty dwellers, so early in the morning—came to Irene across the hazy distance as a low, monotonous hum.

She squinted her eyes and made out a young man taking a Villager's Bath next to his cardboard house—he was dousing himself with water from a tin pail, just as her guidebook promised she might see,

provided she got off the beaten path. She suspected that her guidebook purposefully highlighted strange items then inserted them into
things more normal so that readers would not know which was what.
The Villager's Bath, for example, was tucked in among sections on
Table Etiquette and Insurgent Activity.

Her guidebook seemed to expect things of her. It made her feel
wanting.

If you prefer adventure, you will love this trip.

Hadn't she heard Ron use this very sentence? She had set aside
her *Go Now! - Asia*, which rarely predicted wholeheartedly loving
anything, everything being already semi-trashed. She was back to
reading the service manual.

The youth across the way was a blur. But she could see him
clearly in her mind's eye as he performed his morning ablutions in the
brightening sunlight, which would soon be infused with humidity.
She saw him as shoeless, with rolled up pants, and his chest was bare.

If/seaside/not forget/sunscreen

Enough of the conditional. On to a section called Complaints.

"Choose one of these areas of complaints," the book commanded.
"Or invent your own."

dirty room
bad/slow service
bed too small
noisy room
rude staff

She was hungry. They must be serving breakfast by now. Irene
went back inside and down to the elevator. The cavernous ground
floor had the dead air quality of a soundproof room. Wool carpets
from India and Pakistan were draped in an overlapping sales display
extending out onto the regular carpet. Moss-colored stairways spi-
raled from the lobby floor toward high, chandelier-adorned ceilings.
Up there under the eaves birds were chirping. They were there every
day, an odd detail, especially in the mornings and in the evenings,
when the birds especially fluttered and called.

Irene saw more birds as she entered the empty dining room. They were perched on the ledges of the long windows, or hopping about, looking for crumbs under the tables. Surely, they weren't part of this new hotel's design. Maybe they got in during construction and never got out.

birds in dining room
too many carpets
hotel cold/quiet

A frantic mosquito whined in her ear. She batted it away. A smiling, uniformed youngster glided over to fill her coffee cup in response to this gesture. He had glossy black hair and looked as if he were wearing mascara. The cream color of his jacket matched Irene's large napkin, which was heavy, like a lap robe. She sipped her coffee and returned to *Enjoy Your Stay*. She was the first of the contingent to arrive this morning. She didn't want to look unoccupied.

You are the guest. You are extremely angry. The Complaints section continued.

You think about
a) **what exactly is wrong.**
b) **what you expected.**
c) **what you want to happen now.**

The Unitarians were arriving, always up earlier than the PARADISE crew. They also seemed generally more fit. They filled bowls with oatmeal or soybean porridge and bypassed the other heaped and steaming chafing dishes that encircled the ice sculpture swan.

The Unitarians' daily excursions seemed to be more educational, as well. Today they were going to visit a defunct refugee camp. Some of the refugees who once lived in the camp were now accountants and stockbrokers in Seattle, and that was a fact. The Unitarians thought this a good thing to be made known; it put the lie to those initial flurries of local resistance which gave rise to malicious rumors about the refugees. (Drugs, gangs, stolen puppies, poppies grown for opium in freeway medians, frozen dog carcasses sold to Asian restaurants, government handouts, jobs taken from hard-working

Americans, and so on and so on.) But the Unitarians also felt nostalgic, some of them, for the days when the refugees first came and lived in the church basement and had to be taught so many things.

The group was soon surrounded by more beaming boys wearing the thick, brass-buttoned waiter vestments, their faces wearing the famous Villager's Smile, a collective rictus of cheer. The staff to patron ratio was approximately three to one. This was a ghost hotel, it occurred to Irene, and it was eerie. She remembered what she had read in the English language newspaper—that there were too many new hotels in this city, that on top of skeletal structures there were huge cranes poised mid-swing, indefinitely at rest.

City sidewalks, busy sidewalks, dressed in holiday style...

Recordings of schoolchildren singing Christmas carols in English echoed throughout the dining room. They also played in the lobby and even in the bathrooms. The songs were incongruous to the climbing heat and humidity beyond the windows, but appropriate to the hotel's glacial, climate-controlled air.

The tempos were all the same, the voices, even with discernible accents, seemed computerized. It was a repeating loop, with "Silver Bells" coming up every third song.

People walking, people talking, meeting smile after smile...

accessibility, p. 15

accommodations, p. 160

additional extras, p. 164

Irene was back to *Go Now! – Asia*, skimming. She had forgotten a sweater or shawl and was shivering.

arts and crafts (buying), p. 6, 78, 189

One bird monotonously beat its wings against the glass of first this window, then that, looking for an opening, any small aperture, still hoping to fly out into the hot and noisy world.

14.

The Aliens Among Us
Denise

It was her last day of work, although she didn't know that. She was talking to Tommy Boy, who was mooning around the cash register, right at the start of the shift. She was trying not to picture his teeth. He had a problem with saliva. He didn't seem to feel the need to deal with it. I can't think of the words, he was saying. I can't think to say it. Are you...? What's that ring you're wearing? He finally blurted this sentence, his voice buzzing through his mask. Is it from your boyfriend? Is it from Jimi?

No, she said. Anita wants you, she said. Go talk to Anita.

She pulled out the mirror she kept under the counter and checked her lips. The beauty consultant at Nordstrom gave Denise an extra set. She drew them right around the lips she already had. They were supposed to make her own look fuller, but it looked instead like she was wearing two pairs. It looked like she had a mouth within a mouth.

Jimi said a mouth within a mouth was a sign you were an alien. He showed her a flyer a guy was handing out over near the community college. The aliens among us, the flyer said, can be detected by the fact that they have a mouth within a mouth. The flyers had blurry photos of sample aliens. One was Dan Rather, and another was Martha Stewart. You could sort of see it.

She blinked at herself in the mirror. Sometimes her eyes stung and she had to blink a lot. Tommy Boy would ask her then why she was crying. I'm not, she'd say. I'm just wearing mascara, which can give you pink eye.

People might describe a woman or girl as not pretty but beautiful, but she was neither. Maybe she was cute. That was possible. She examined the back of her head from time to time in a mirror. Or she looked at herself face on, quick, trying to get a fresh perspective. But in the end, she didn't care about cute. Cute was a quantity, like pretty. You were more or less cute, more or less pretty. Scale of 1 to 10.

She wanted to be beautiful. She wanted to be touched by beauty, marked by it. Stricken. She wanted to be like Snow White—dead, when the prince first meets her. Beauty embalmed. She wanted it out of her hands.

Tommy Boy always told her she was pretty. She felt his wistful gaze. She was the only one from the regular staff who ever listened to him talk. The pizza boys just snorted and laughed and filled the orders. Sixteen pepperoni on a medium, twenty-four on a large. They had to count it out each time, they couldn't tell by looking.

Tommy Boy showed up for work on foot carrying his costume in a paper sack, mouse ears sticking out of the top. He rode the city bus to the stop three blocks away. He had his schedule all worked out, he'd repeat it to you. He came plenty early to get ready. Denise figured he thought they were stars, he and Anita, when they put on those masks and danced out under the pipe organ, Mickey and Minnie, all the colored lights whirling and the bubbles spewing from the bubble machine.

It was the pizza boys who started calling him "Tommy Boy." They'd zing an empty pizza box at him, which he'd catch in the stomach. And then it was like the smile on his mask went slack. His teeth, Denise could just guess, were wet.

The pizza boys talked to each other through Tommy Boy. They said How's it goin? What's happenin? Whadaya say? Gettin any? Okay, nothing, not much, no, he answered. Then he searched the words for the meaning. The pizza boys screwed up their curly lips and talked sideways. Or they managed to make their lips not move at all.

Brittany, Bethany, and Brianna never talked to Tommy Boy. They stood stoic at their cash registers, each in the droopy, red corduroy cap, the big red bowtie, the striped smock with the monkey applique on the back. They were high school seniors who only talked amongst themselves. There'd been another "B" –Bridget, Burgundy, or something, but she became "with kid" (as Jimi called it) and quit.

The three B's punched in the orders, took the money, and said "Thank yew!!" like somebody pulled a string.

Mr. Mancey walked through the work station every night nodding to the B's and the pizza boys, saying: How's it going? What's happenin? Whadaya say? Everyone answered: Okay, nothing, not much. Then the pizza boys snorted and laughed.

Mr. Mancey wore a green suit jacket and a maroon tie and tight pants over his ample tush and a thick wedding ring and a name tag bigger than anybody's with a bigger organ logo. He had an old permanent in his dirty red hair. He played the big guy to Denise. He tapped her resume with a pencil when he hired her and said: What's a facilitator? Like it was French. He wanted to know about the Shoot for the Stars workshop ("Shoot the stars!" Jimi called it), like maybe he thought Denise was making it up. He said: What's a Care Co-Aide? About her month with Mr. Simms. He said: What's this three-year gap?

She got one dollar above minimum wage and no tips. Head cashier, big fucking deal. BFD. Thank god for her mom, good old mom. And her dad, ol' deadbeat. But not that *re*tard Jimi, the person she was supposed to be escaping from right now this very minute on her trip, her fabulous PARADISE PROMISE of Amazing Asia!

Denise's mom worked for RealRoutes in the Portland office, downtown. She set up the tours, the Amazing! whatevers. Every time Denise's mom heard Jimi was hanging around again looking evil (his specialty), she sent Denise somewhere warm. She gave her vitamins. She said Denise did not want to compromise her future. She gave her herbal remedies. She said the company we keep says a lot about ourselves. She said Denise should take notes. On the tour, not on Jimi. She wanted her to go to tour school or whatever. Forget it, Denise said. I am nowhere near Amazing! enough.

Mr. Mancey said, being real friendly, that they were all Pipe Organ People, the pizza boys and her and Tommy and Giggles, which is what he called Anita, who always did then, she giggled, like clockwork. But he wanted to make them pay for the fact that he wasn't a doctor or a lawyer or a stockbroker at Piper, Jaffray, and BFD. He was just the manager at Pipe Organ Pizza, with the two-story pipe organ and fifty kinds of pizza. He wasn't Amazing! at all.

~

Jimi was named for Jimi Hendrix. His mom was a biker. He'd been a biker baby. His dad was dead. Viet Nam. Kapowie. The last year of the war, the last month, maybe even the very last day. Maybe even the very last bullet, the last piece of shrapnel. It had to be someone, didn't it? The last casualty. Shit happens.

Jimi's mom would show up, then she'd go away.

"She comes and goes with the buffaloes," said Jimi, who claimed he was part Cherokee. Mostly she'd go. She'd be totally gone, "in every sense of the word," said Jimi, who was pretty smart, even if he didn't always act it. Pretty smart and pretty old to be still trying to figure out how to eat.

He hung around a lot at "the Organ" (his term), at least he did before Denise escaped to PARADISE. See you at the Organ, he'd say. I just love the Organ, don't you? That's what he'd say. He pretended to be thrilled when Mickey and Minnie did the Disney Dance every hour at quarter past. Denise thought that maybe he really was sort of thrilled.

It was certainly a big deal for Tommy Boy and Anita. They waited in the wings, which just meant they stood against the wall by the cash registers in full view of the customers filing in, but out of sight of the customers eating pizza out on the floor beneath the giant organ. They'd stand there by the customer line being Mickey and Minnie and waving back and forth, back and forth, while handing out flyers for delivery specials. When the time drew near, Tommy Boy would straighten the flounces of Anita's frock, per her muffled directions, and she'd fuss with her gloves, they would really get into it and act nervous. Then at a quarter past the hour organist Terrance Tawney would play a big Tah-Da! chord and they'd do the Disney Dance, skipping out among the tables as if they'd found their long-lost playmates. Even though everyone eating pizza had already seen them.

Anita arrived at work in her full Minnie getup, including the large white gloves and the little black purse and the shiny Minnie shoes. The van from Living Alternatives dropped her off. She even wore her mask. She looked like a large trick-or-treater, sitting there in the way back seat. No one knew what all she kept in that purse. Nothing, maybe. It was just part of the costume. It was Minnie's.

Sometimes Mr. Mancey came in with his wife Melinda, looking large and sleepy because she was pregnant. (He called her Belinda, for some reason, maybe because of Brittany-Bethany-Brianna, and the pizza boys called her Beluga.) They would eat a pizza out at the tables, and Anita would hang around them, her masked breath heavy and moist. You're eating for two, Anita would splutter. Make sure you feed that baby! Mr. Mancey teased her about getting a baby of her own. He said Go for it, Giggles! and she giggled, right on schedule, the sound a big gulp behind the happy Minnie face.

~

The extra lips were drawn on with a Rosy Quartz 06 pencil, then filled in with Moon Glow. All of it Quintessence. She could only afford the lipstick that time because she was saving up for her tattoo, which

Jimi had said he would do at a discount. Plus, she wanted to get some of the Body Balm. Either that or the Moisture Lush face cream, designed to smooth out fine wrinkles and marionette lines, according to the beauty consultant, who pointed at invisible vertical indentations on her own face. The Body Balm came in a pink frosted jar with a lid shaped like a big seashell. When the beauty consultant screwed open the jar it made the slurping sound jars with expensive stuff make.

A man with long, pale fingers and a leather bracelet smoothed the lotion on the back of his hand while Denise was having her makeover. She couldn't move her head, so she only saw his fingers and the bracelet. Does it plump up? He asked. He smelled good. Denise wanted to look at his face but couldn't, because it was time for her eyes.

She wanted the Body Balm because of the jar, and she wanted the tattoo to affix herself permanently in youthful beauty (as Jimi so fancily put it), as well as to exile herself forever from certain kinds of lives (as Jimi proposed), lives that required a totally normal appearance. Plus, she just thought it might look good, a little spider on her neck, just below her earlobe. Jimi said he could do that. He said it would be like an accessory. Set off her features in a very cool way. You could tell he was practicing his tattoo talk for his customers, once he ever got any.

Organist Terrance Tawney didn't appear to have a tattoo, but he had a full-on mullet. No one saw him up close, because he never took his breaks. He just scooted into the men's room and returned all slicked back. He never collected his allotted Little Monkey's pizza or salad. He didn't even swipe a cracker from the salad bar and this was in a six-hour shift, three to nine. Yet he was very pudgy. He bounced around on that bench and did his tap dance on the pedals, but other than that Denise guessed there wasn't much exercise playing the organ.

When organist Terence Tawney first got to work he walked directly from his dented Mazda in the parking lot to the front doors of the building, passing the poster that showed him baring his teeth. He glanced at the poster, checked to see if that was still him, and then he hustled straight to the high, polished organ bench, nodding right and left to nobody in particular. He wore the same mustard-colored suit jacket every day, with a striped tie and a dingy old white shirt pulled tight over his paunch. If there were people already on the floor eating their pizza, he gave them a bug-eyed stare that possibly was supposed to be a pleasant hello, before he slid around and pulled out the stops.

Once Denise saw him coming out of the McDonald's on 82nd late in the evening. She was on the bus, the 10:20. He stopped on the sidewalk with his hands in his jacket pockets and just stood there, angled out toward the street, his head illuminated in the glow of the golden arches, his face cocked sideways and up, like he was listening to some terrific story. His pug nose and those round cheeks were all red and sweaty between the retro sideburns. He was smiling and nodding, all by himself, and his mullet was getting matted from the rain.

Another time she spied him arranging his face in his car out in the parking lot. He had the rearview mirror angled and was choosing his entry expression. Pleasant, yes, and slightly surprised. Rushed, pressed, many engagements. But pleased to have been asked to play.

When organist Terence Tawney played "Take Me Out to the Ball Game," no. 12 on the Old Favorites list, that was the cue for Tommy Boy and Anita to get ready. They gave themselves plenty of prep time. They stood still and thought about their characters. "Take Me Out to the Ball Game" was the only Old Favorite that no one ever requested, but it was always right before the Disney Dance tune, which was "It's a Small World, After All."

During the Small song, Mickey and Minnie were supposed to shake hands with the customers. This was something that Tommy Boy and Anita could really get worked up about. They'd stop on a dime, mid-prance, clap their heels together and bow like robots, elbows clamped to their waists, hand-shaking hands jutting straight out. They only did this for the little ones, though, the real little kids, like two-year-olds, maybe, or any nice-seeming grandmas. Because older kids sometimes made fun of them. Even grownups.

~

One day they were getting ready for the Disney Dance and Anita was bowing her head like she was praying, and Tommy Boy was squaring his shoulders, pulling at the chin of this mask, positioning it over and over, his nervous tic. There was a lull in her line of customers, three large families were shuffling on to Brittany, Bethany, and Brianna. Denise decided to straighten out and bundle her bills, which were piling up. It had been a busy day. All of the bills had to be face up and the heads of Washington, Lincoln, or whoever had to be pointing up and down the same way. When she got them all organized, she'd take a little key from underneath the money tray, unlock the drawer below the register, take out the canvas Seafirst Bank bag, deposit the bundle o' money, zip it back up, put it back in the drawer and lock it, put back the key.

Usually she had this down to a one-minute routine, but that time she couldn't find the little key. Jimi was distracting her, hanging over the counter and punching the buttons on Ye Olde Cash Register. They had to use old-timey brass contraptions, like everyone stuffing their faces with pizza in front of a giant organ with big, dancing rodents was quaint as hell.

So she was sweeping her hand underneath the cash carrier, only getting paper clips and rubber bands and personal checks with all those different designs on them, scenery and ducks and shit. Some teenage boys came up to the register while she was riffling around this way, hoping Mr. Mancey wasn't looking at her clutching that big wad of cash. And the teenagers were all ordering at once and she said "One moment please," and they kept on ordering. They said "Gimme the Orangutan," like it was a big joke instead of just the menu. They turned to each other and said, "Gimme the King of the Jungle," and hooted like morons. Denise said, "I'll be right with you," and they sang "Taaake me out and let's ball, babe," tossing crumpled-up flyers onto the half-prepared pizzas of the pizza boys, who snorted and laughed.

Finally, she found that goddamn key down in the pocket of her monkey smock where she kept her herbal remedies. It was caught in Kleenex, she couldn't believe it. She couldn't believe she was almost crying. What was *wrong* with her? She should just smack those little piss-ants.

She unlocked the drawer and grabbed the bank bag, and then she couldn't find the bunch of bills. She must have put it down somewhere, holy shit. She said to the idiot boys, "I'll be right with you," using her best fake voice, and they milled around, slamming each other into the wall. Then Jimi, who'd been lounging all over the counter laughing, got the good idea to tease Anita, showing off for the youngsters. Anita came out of her prayer state just in time to see Jimi's hand heading for the polka dot bow on her head. She clamped both of her hands over the bow, and over his hand, too, and their hands tussled up there on her head for a bit, becoming all wrapped up together. Anita couldn't seem to let go. Finally, one of her white gloves came off in Jimi's hand. Tommy Boy was just standing there, holding his mask by the chin, the tips of his fingers on that big, insane grin.

Jimi got real embarrassed then, everyone seeing him tangling hands like that with Minnie. And Jimi embarrassed was sort of ugly. He swore at Anita and yanked his hand away and threw down the glove like it was infected. Then he headed out the door and the pizza boys were hooting and Denise could hear Anita crying with big, coughing sounds behind her mask.

~

When Jimi skedaddled that day, he called back "Later!" and "Tattoo night! Don't fergit!" He had some stuff he'd been all cagey about, too, something or other they were going to do, good shit, he said, expensive as hell. He'd made her pay half and she didn't even know what it was, what kind of big treat she was in for. That was Jimi. Half her paycheck seemed to go to Jimi. He'd say something was all whoop-ti-do, and they'd take it and—nothing. Expensive as hell,

every time, could she pay half? Denise suspected they were tripping
on vitamins.

Anyway, that was her last day of work, as it turned out, in a week
that involved the police coming to the house along with Mr. Mancey,
who accused her of stealing from the till, and then the police wanting Jimi's full name and address, and her mom getting all freaked
out, and Denise puking all over her mom's new couch from Ikea.
Then there was a hearing, plea bargain, whatchacallit, and the first
exciting preparations for a glorious SuperValue Chartered Quest to
parts unknown. Denise's mom drove her up to SeaTac just to make
sure Denise got on the flight, and even ol' deadbeat Dad came along,
telling his department chair he had jury duty. Everything, except the
police and the puking, so very familiar.

~

Anita's bow ended up crooked on that eventful day, but by God
she had it. When she stopped crying, she slid an old compact and
lipstick out of her pinafore pocket. She pulled her mask out to a
45-degree angle and did a quick check on her lips. She liked to keep
them smeared with bright red lipstick, even though no one saw them.
Mr. Mancey came over, wiping his mouth with a napkin. The teenagers had moved on and were sprawled up and down the big table right
under the organ. Mr. Mancey told Anita to keep her white gloves on
at all times while on the floor. She nodded and nodded, her mask
going up and down, then she and Tommy Boy held hands and started
waving, waiting for the umpteenth verse of the "It's a Small World"
so they could start out just right for the big prance.

Denise's eyes were getting blurry. Her eye shadow was making
her lids itch. The Small Song began and churned away. Sometimes she
liked to keep her brains straight by punching out the orders in tempo.
She'd take an herbal remedy and then she'd punch away. Except for
the on-the-hour "Theme from 2001: A Space Odyssey," organist Terence Tawney played every song at the exact same speed and all of

them, especially the Space Odyssey Theme, *fortissimo fff!* He played that giant two-story organ like it was a John Deere tractor and he was working his way around the field, getting in the crops. When he was done playing, that was that, hop off the seat, out the door.

The soggy light in the parking lot began to fade. *Keep your future wide open.* That's what her mom loved to say. Denise could see her reflection in the far window, moving here, moving there, like a puppet. *Don't do something you will later regret.* Rain made the pavement shiny. It was warm inside the Organ, yeasty-smelling from all that dough, everything a bright orange. The parking lot began to disappear, and her reflection grew clear. She could see her big, red, corduroy hat bobbing around like a poppy.

She'd get another makeover, get some Quintessence shit. Body splash, maybe. Because skin can forget to function. Cosmetologists will tell you that. They'll give you pamphlets. Note your skin's behavior, the pamphlets say. Is your skin sluggish? Overstimulated? Does it need comforting? Irrigation? There's a cascade of ongoing negative effects. You must hydrate, feed, firm, and protect your skin, while refreshing its moisture memory. Underneath the skin you see is the skin you want.

The glow outside turned fast to black. Behind their masks, Anita's lips were brilliant and Tommy Boy's teeth were glistening. Mr. Mancey and Melinda/Belinda wiped their mouths and just at that moment the pizza boys burst out laughing. Denise blinked and said "Thank yew!!" like somebody pulled a string.

15.
Alone

In an effort to be friendly, Irene was sharing aloud sections of the English language newspaper with the woman with the beaded bracelets, who wrote rapidly in her trip journal, her "log," as she called it.

"Globalize Dessert?" Irene uttered doubtfully, misreading a brandished sign in a photo accompanying an article about a protest in Seattle.

"Dissent! Dissent!" the woman with the bracelets (Monica something) corrected, without humor, snapping shut her notebook. "Dissent!" she repeated impatiently, causing the others to stop eating and stare.

It was the morning of Day 08. Enmities were starting to arise. Mrs. Small was curt with Keith, something to do with attire. Mr. Small was dissatisfied with Ron's guiding style, he said Ron should provide more information about his home life, offer himself up as a sort of representative case from the local culture.

Irene was embarrassed to find herself blinking back tears behind her newspaper, which she held up high. Such a sharp response to a simple sharing of information seemed hurtful. It *was* hurtful. Irene felt that she had been friendly with this Monica—she of the bracelets, as the elderly man in the bolo tie referred to her. He had shared with Monica his own name, but she never used it. In their occasional one-on-one exchanges Maxwell S. Edgars went missing. He was just a guy, he supposed, tucking and re-tucking his napkin. An old guy.

Denise had abandoned Irene long ago. Irene thought they might sit together at meal times, since they were roommates, but Denise always made a beeline for some other table. Granted, Denise hardly spoke with anyone associated with the tour except Pete. Denise and Pete might banter for a bit about the food items and the decorations on the breakfast buffet.

Sometimes Pete bantered with Irene, too, but she suspected that it was at her expense. He tended to repeat phrases she used in a way that made her think he might be laughing at her. The fall colors, for example. She told him about all the fall colors that were so wonderful in a pamphlet about a scenic tour to New England some members of her church group might someday take. Why repeat it back to her as if it were strange?

Maybe it was just the weepy time of the trip. She had thought to find new friends, but was finding no one congenial. She didn't know when, exactly, she had started to use words like that, careful words like "congenial." *Congenital?* She could hear Herbert's voice. Which made her want to weep even more.

Keith, at least, was always polite to Irene, if in a strained way. The sharing of esoteric medical conditions helped. He told her he had an essential tremor and they had a good laugh trying to say "cerebellum," which Keith pronounced with a bit of a lisp. Mr. and Mrs. Small made her feel single. They were nice enough, although today they looked atypically cranky and were behaving in an extra-exaggeratedly polite manner toward one another.

Irene thought the Smalls must have a nice life there in Seattle. They'd shared some interesting facts with her about the traffic and the bridges and Chinatown. And the fish! She asked them if they bought fish at the Pike's Place Market or at the supermarket, and they said both. She confessed to them that she thought that must be nice, buying fresh fish any old where. She said that she used to get fresh fish when Fred was alive, of course, but... They didn't inquire. She confessed to them that Seattle held a certain draw for her, although the traffic must be just terrible. And she wasn't sure she could live in all that rain.

She just guessed she was a drylander, Irene called out to the Smalls, as they exited the dining area. She guessed she was a prairie gal, she said to her newspaper, holding it up again and snapping the pages.

16.

To the Coast!

Irene

Her earliest memory of going to Seattle was marked by the trees west of Spokane. They bordered both sides of both parts of the freeway—the two lanes coming east, appearing from time to time through the pines like a river, and the two lanes going west, the path that irrevocably held Irene and her family, in the large, cream-colored Plymouth station wagon with dual expanses of hot, sticky, davenport seats. There was a third, queasy seat facing backwards, and from this Irene and her brothers and sisters took turns waving goodbye to the long, lonely plains and the few cars they passed.

If she were to examine this memory more closely Irene would realize that their car left the arid plains and entered lush forests long before Spokane. And then, just west of Spokane, after that last little garden of trees, they were out on the plains again. Those plains, though, were different from the ones Irene was used to. Those plains seemed prehistoric, dead, devoid of even the memory of life. They were inert. Why?

Maybe it was the freeway. All motion was sucked out of the plains and funneled onto the freeway, with its generous shoulders, lavish medians, and exits swirling to rest areas as roomy and pleasant as city parks. The thin line US Hwy 2 drew across the top of Montana seemed stiff and dry by comparison. But the plains back home, the vast expanse stretching east from the Rockies, those plains were alive, they continually whispered and groaned.

Irene barely sensed this difference when she was young. And there actually hadn't been such things as rest areas then, or if there were, she didn't remember them. Her family always stopped at the ice cream stand in St. Regis and this had the same gooey-topped tables and fly-haunted garbage cans as the Tastee Freez in Arboleda. Maybe that tree-lined strip of freeway heading west from Spokane was just a long driveway that became, in her imagination, the grand approach to somebody's palace, somebody who lived in Seattle. The plains part that followed had the static feeling of a foyer, a waiting room. Irene didn't pay much attention to the actual terrain.

There were cousins who lived "on the coast," as Irene liked to say. These cousins belonged to a moderately-sized family of four. Irene's uncle, her mother's brother, had lived with Aunt Peggy in Dickinson, North Dakota, where he worked in the post office. But he had in mind a different life, evidenced by the fact that he drove a sports car. Once, when Irene was so small she could see only the odd-knobbed door handle and rubber floor pads, he gave her a ride. Then he and Peggy were off for the coast.

Irene's family told a story about how this aunt and uncle, having escaped from Dickinson and moved almost to Seattle, took their children to see *Lawrence of Arabia* on Christmas Eve instead of staying home waiting for Santa. This may have happened just the one time, but the fact seemed to Irene as a child outwardly wonderful and secretly bleak. She felt that Seattle might demand commitments from her she couldn't make.

Two children. Irene knew that her aunt and uncle had only two children by choice. Children by choice. Her aunt and uncle, and possibly her cousins, too, would go to Limbo when they died. They weren't Catholics was why. Her uncle had been Catholic, but he'd fallen away. *Fallen away.* It sounded so graceful and sad.

Irene and her family didn't go to church every single Sunday, truth be told. They might grant themselves special dispensations (the weather, the work, the wind . . .). They ate fish sticks on Fridays, though, and they knew how to say an Act of Contrition. They knew about Limbo, which wasn't doing a back bend under a broomstick. Limbo was a vague place drained of all motion and hue, just like those plains west of Spokane. And Seattle, in Irene's mind, was heaven.

Her relatives hadn't quite made it. When they moved to the city, they settled just short of the bridge spanning Lake Washington, in an innocuous suburb of glassy office complexes and shopping malls and streets with no sidewalks. Still, this place came just before Seattle on the freeway going west. There, on the ocean side of the Cascades, Irene felt she had crossed some divide of difference. And there her anxieties set in.

They mostly had to do with her pants, or maybe her dress, or sometimes her shoes, any of which might be newly-purchased for the trip and, though glowing with promise in Arboleda and out on the ranch, now all wrong. It had nothing to do with fashion, it had to do with fit. Not the way the clothes fit Irene, the way she fit the world. The cosmos. She expected the clothes, purchased for travel, to change her. Of course, this would not happen all of a sudden or even over a period of time, if that time were spent at home. It was a combination of things that would do it, an alchemy of color, motion, and place. The new clothes moving through space, mixed with Seattle, and applied to her body. She would be transformed.

One year she wore red shoes. She loved them instantly when first strapping them on at the Fashion Shoppe in Crag. The shoes were flat, oval-toed, and pewter-buckled, befitting any competent and attractive heroine, the kind Irene read about in books with titles like *The Mystery of Slippery Rock Lagoon*. There were reservoirs near Arboleda, but no lagoons that she knew of. Neither was there an old mill stream, but that did not stop Irene from imagining one when she and Herbert sang about it, a mill stream with hanging moss.

She sang lots of crazy duets with her brother Herbert on trips to Seattle.

Down by the old ... (not the new, but the old!) ... *mill* ... *stream* (not the river, but the stream!) ... *where I first* ... (not last, but first!) *met* ... *you* (not me, but you!)

On the tops of the red shoes were three holes the size and shape of pumpkin seeds, arranged in a crescent. These struck Irene as frivolous and daring, the cleft of her toes just barely revealed. Another interesting feature was the incorporation of two kinds of leather—soft suede for the front half (you could brush it this way and that and make shadows) and even softer, buttery leather for the back half that would have felt, if Irene had known to make the comparison, as smooth as the inside of her upper thigh. Best of all was the color. Crimson red.

Because these shoes were flat and buckled, they were deceptively conservative. They reminded Irene of an old Audrey Hepburn movie she'd seen on her family's new Zenith TV. Audrey's character worked in a bookstore and wore ostensibly frumpy, but actually form-fitting tweed skirts and high-necked white cotton blouses and absurd horn-rimmed glasses, and all of this seemingly allowed her to be innocent of who she actually was—a devastating beauty of quiet power, linked to another world. Irene's red shoes, she liked to think, would give her that kind of power, as they carried her first to Seattle and then back home and down the halls of Arboleda Junior High.

In a photo taken at the Seattle Center and preserved behind wrinkled cellophane in a family photo album, Irene wore an olive-green dress with a red plaid bow tie and Peter Pan collar and three inches of slip showing. Irene and her siblings all dressed up like this for the city. A white cloth headband firmly covered her ears and cinched in her part (she was trying to grow out her bangs), and she dangled her first big lady purse self-consciously, as if it were a two-pound trout. And, too tight with modest socks on, she wore those shoes. She was smiling wanly, and thinking about a drowning, the aftermath of which she had just witnessed.

They had taken the train that time. It was August. Irene and Viva
and Herbert left Dad and Melvin to finish haying. The Big Girls were
at 4-H camp, a bunch of hyped-up teenagers and a few half-hearted
counselors in a cluster of tipis near the cottonwood grove on McAl-
pin's Reservoir, forty miles north of Arboleda. Doreen and Carleen
reported, via a hand-delivered letter addressed to Viva (FYEO—For
Your Eyes Only!!), that Indian girls from the Job Corps, working as
cooks at the camp, had threatened to beat them up. The letter lan-
guished on the kitchen table for the week of their mother's absence,
waiting to deliver its guilt-inducing message upon her return. (The
Big Girls were jealous that Herbert and Little Sister got to take a train
trip to the city, while they themselves were forced to spend their days
learning how to tie a tourniquet and apply first aid treatment for bee
stings.) Doreen and Carleen wrote that they told the Indian girls that
their grandfather had once been in love with an Indian named Maggie, but the girls just said, "No shit." This response was not reported
exactly. The letter stated that the Indian girls said they didn't care.

Viva had made plans for the train trip to cheer up Herbert, who was
having a bad summer for no specific reason. He was just down. She was
carrying out the travel plans, haying or no haying, Big Girls belly-aching
or not. They all three shared a private compartment with adjoining bath,
Herbert on the top bunk, Viva and Irene down below. Dad said he didn't
want them to have to sleep sitting up, and the meals came with.

Irene was luxuriating in her sister-less status, the banishment
of The Big Girls. At the same time, she was feeling an unusual pressure of her mother's attention. This was not inspired by anything
Viva was actually doing. Viva was only reading aloud sections from
House Beautiful, articles on various uses for adhesive tape and tips for
washing wallpaper. (*Overlap your strokes and proceed with great care, or
the wall will look streaky.*) Herbert lay on the top bunk looking out the
window. Viva and Irene had to hunker over a little, underneath. They
had wanted to postpone having the top bunk lowered until after dinner, but Herbert wanted to lie down right away, so they said Oh fine.

Except for being so tired, Herbert already seemed a little more like his good old self. He offered some suggestions for adhesive tape, which Viva ignored. She turned to look out the window, when they stopped at towns, putting down her magazine. She said she liked to watch the family goodbyes on the platforms of all the little towns the train passed—the "butt ends" of the towns, she pointed out, the tracks seeming always to flow along bar street. Families were sending their kids off to college early to get settled. Moms and Dads and siblings and old grandparents clustered around the young travelers, who clutched pillows and large bags of pretzels or licorice and tried with difficulty to keep their faces nonchalant. People stood on the platforms and stared up at the train, and when it began to move they took a step back. They waved to the passengers, trying to make their own faces positive. Off to Northern Montana College in Havre, off to beauty school or Kinman Business College in Spokane. The time of life when leaving really does matter, when you send someone permanently away, or when you leave someone—yourself—behind forever.

Viva supposed that most people going as far as Seattle these days might choose to fly. This she decided after asking a number of passengers in the dining car their destinations.

It wasn't anything that Viva was doing that bothered Irene. It was just that Irene was used to keeping company with her mother's oblique, erratically-expressed love, not addressing it. She liked being parallel, not face on. In the small, strange train compartment, she felt oddly shy. She felt as if she had a houseguest inside her body. Even before the train left Montana, she, too, was tired. She had been so excited. Now she just wanted to say "Love ya," and head out the door to somewhere regular, like the school bus.

Irene and Viva had their books and magazines; Herbert had a toy gun. At fourteen, he was certainly too old for a toy gun, but it was a new prop for his jokey personality and for a determinedly blithe, smooth persona that he'd developed just for the trip. He needed it. That whole past year he had become unfathomably sad. He was handsome and athletic and musical, but he couldn't seem to join in, not the way he was expected to in a small town that was ready to make him its next hero. He quit freshman football. He played an old, beat-up guitar in the family room. He tried pacing among the parked cars outside the gym during the basketball games with the hoods and hippies and a handful of renegade Indians. Arboleda wouldn't let him diverge; this excursion into the town's countercultures became just another dimension of his preordained fate there as Most All Around.

Herbert had worked out an approach to Irene for the trip that involved calling her "Chlorine" and also "Sis," which she especially did not like. "Sis" was so distancing and so somehow defeating. When he did that they were just pretend siblings of the most mundane variety—Trixie Belden, a spunky, curly-haired, serialized child-sleuth and her Hardy Boy brother. Those preteen, paperback children didn't live the wonderful, marginal life of Nancy Drew (who lived in Irene's hardbound collection, which Herbert also enjoyed), or of Joan of Arc, who was someone Irene found attractive, if intimidating.

In Arboleda, any yen for the wild and powerful was restricted to emblematic animals. Irene and her sisters belonged to the Soaring Eagles 4-H Club. (Head, heart, hands, and . . . what else? Irene never could remember.) Melvin and Herbert had been Arboleda Junior High Cougars, in preparation for becoming Arboleda High School Warriors, the insignia on the team jackets a war bonnet. ("Indians shouldn't be mascots, they are not animals, nor something archaic," said the new principal, who soon moved on.) Melvin was a Warrior only for a while, then he devoted his rare free time to local rodeo bulldogging and bronc riding. Herbert devoted his time to sitting inside complaining. And playing that beat up guitar.

For a very brief period that nobody mentioned, Dad attempted to become an Elk, whispering lines for a secret ceremony while curry-combing his rope horse, Mike. Occasionally, Viva played Round Robin bridge, driving into town on a Tuesday night, and she belonged to Cow Belles, a rural-based civic organization that provided potluck casseroles at jackpot ropings. Even if flower clubs had existed in Arboleda, Viva would not have joined. Her indoor flowers, her "kids," were her very own thing.

Irene felt that they—she—could be part of something more. She went through a spell of making noon hour visits to church. This was partly to get warm and out of the wind during the school lunch hour, but she also yearned for (and feared) a vision—a white light and solemn voice, just for her. She wanted to place herself in the path of this possibility, even while maintaining, just a little while longer, the status quo of a vision-less life. She would gaze up like St. Bernadette at the Virgin Mary's plaster sky-blue cloak framing her downcast face, enjoying the imagined tableau. But she responded to the church's bated breath with: "Not today, please, please, no visions today, *thank you,* I love you, I love you, amen."

She tried to read the Bible, all on her own. Catholics never read the Bible, in her experience, they just memorized the Baltimore Catechism. *Who made you? God made you! Who is God? God is a Supreme Being who something, something, something!* The cadence was like the pep club cheers. The Bible, on the other hand, had characters and stories. But making her way through the odd language, the comings and goings, the affronts and sacrifices, she'd arrive, abruptly, at a dead end. The prodigal son comes home, and his Dad is glad to see him. Fact. This happens. End of story. Why did he go away in the first place? It seemed unclear.

She could detect lessons lurking in history class, yet Irene felt only faintly impressed at the lurid pictures in the textbook of voyages, discoveries, Christopher Columbus, Captain Cook, Lewis and Clark. Inspiration was to be drawn from those watery expeditions and those tedious upriver portages, but—other than bull-headed determination—what? She wasn't sure. Far off on a ridgeline there were a couple Indians watching Lewis and Clark from horseback, in the textbook illustration, their dogs watching, too. The Indians' hair was blown back, and they wore simple pants, shirts, and moccasins, just everyday clothes, their work outfits. They looked interested, but busy. They had no clue as to the shit-show to follow. That's what Herbert once said, in class, and he got a detention.

In bed at night when she was a child, Irene sometimes said a rosary until she fell asleep, waking in the morning with a crucifix mark on her cheek. She was in training for being a saint in heaven. She did not imagine actually being in heaven, she only imagined going there. Herbert would tease her on this point. He'd say, "What'll you do when you get there?" She couldn't explain. Going to heaven was a meteor shower from which one emerged empowered, soaked in strangeness, trans-substantiated, that weird word they learned in Catechism. A consecration of violence. She'd heard a visiting priest say that once in his homily. "Carnations and violets" is what Viva, encouraged by Herbert, thought the priest had said.

~

The train halted in Spokane. There was some activity on the banks of the Spokane River—men were pulling a tarp out of the water onto the opposite bank. Emergency vehicles were parked nearby, doors open. One booted leg flopped out of the tarp. Herbert became excited and Irene quickly looked away. A man had drowned! Why? Had he jumped into the river? Had he been drunk? Confused? Was he pushed? Was it a man at all?

Viva moaned a little in distress. She didn't like human suffering. Well, who the heck did? But Viva was different from many of the wives who lived in greater Arboleda, women who wanted Indians to be white or in jail, women who were death on "two-dollar bills" (the local term for homosexuals), women who snubbed unwed mothers. Just the week previous, while watching a dramatization of the Nuremberg trials on the Zenith, Viva had become very quiet, but she kept watching, and she shed some tears all over her ironing, not even trying to hide them.

Irene understood. She wanted to go out into the world, and she wanted to shatter into stars in heaven, but, more than that, she wanted to stay put in the fold of her mother's arm forever. To go away was to risk never coming back, prodigal or otherwise. This, Irene felt, was the tacit dilemma that she and Viva endured as they read books or magazines next to each other on train trips to Seattle or at home on silent summer nights. They shared the light of one lamp, their eyes on the page, all other sense alert to the outer dark.

"A father was holding the hand of a boy about ten years old, speaking to him softly," the Nuremberg man on TV said. "The boy was fighting his tears. The father pointed toward the sky, stroked his head, and seemed to explain something to him. At that moment, the SS man at the pit shouted something to his comrade. The latter counted off 20 persons and instructed them to go..."

Their train left Spokane and set out over the dead plains. Irene read her book, *The Wolves of Willoughby Chase*, about two orphan girls hiding in a forest, on the run from bad people, surviving by pricking small holes in raw eggs and sucking out the insides. Viva returned to *House Beautiful*, pointing out unlikely valances and wrought iron birdbaths. Herbert resumed playing with his toy gun. The barrel could be pushed in and locked. It popped out sharply when the trigger was pulled. Herbert pushed the barrel in and put it to his temple. Then he leaned over the edge of the bunk and put it to Irene's.

"Thar she blows," he said, and pulled. Irene exploded in pent up tears, her hand to her temple, and fled to the small bathroom, where she cried noisily while Viva checked for blood, and then quietly for many minutes. Finally, Viva said, "You're making your brother feel pretty bum."

And it's true, Herbert was lying on his bunk and staring out the window, and Irene, when she emerged, could see that he was blinking back his own tears. She saw in his face her own confused emotions, and she loved him in a great, rejuvenated rush. She knew in her heart that he had been calling her "Chlorine" and "Sis" in an effort to tamp down fear. He was fourteen, she was almost thirteen, they were dying to their childhoods. Being alive carried a newly precarious weight. She wanted to help him, grab hold of him, but she checked herself. She didn't know why. She was teetering on her own narrow path. Maybe she just didn't want to be distracted.

Irene couldn't get the image of the drowned man's boot out of her mind, and it followed her to Seattle, mixing with the words at Nuremberg and Viva's face and Herbert's teasing and then her tears and his tears and her pinching shoes and Viva saying that she thought that Irene's new bangs made her look a jot like who was it? Audrey Hepburn. Which made Irene want to cry all over again, her mother saying that, because Irene knew she most certainly did not look like Audrey Hepburn, not even close, not one little bit.

~

Then Irene was seventeen. She and Doreen were driving to Seattle. If it was rainy for days on end, or if one big downpour necessitated a wait before baling could begin, or if the baler's regular breakdowns turned into a major one, then Dad might give his hay crew short summer vacations in groups of two. This driving to Seattle to visit their cousins was Irene and Doreen's fortuitous getaway. All they'd been doing was helping Viva some with the cooking, anyway, because of their splenectomies. They were still feeling a little delicate.

Before leaving town, they stopped at the Rexall Drug on Arboleda's main street to buy sunglasses. Irene's were faintly tinged an azure blue. This was the designated fashion color for a pair of sandals she'd brought in Crag that spring to wear to the senior girls' Mother-Daughter banquet at the Elks Club. While everyone ate fruit cocktail, the senior girls sang "Let. There. Be peace. On earth. And let it begin with meeeee....." Three months later, Irene wasn't sure about that color for footwear, but she secretly like its wacky, wild look when applied to her eyes.

Carleen said she felt a little delicate, too, so she spent all her time with her summer boyfriend, Danny. He came out to the ranch in his Camaro and off they went to town, and sometimes to Crag for the whole day.

Irene had started dating Fred, by then, Danny's brother. It all began with a double date, Irene and Fred in the back seat, taking their cues from Danny and Carleen, Irene sipping her beer like it was Alka-Seltzer. She liked Fred, but not in the same way Carleen seemed to like Danny. Something wasn't quite up to par with her and Fred, Irene suspected. They weren't likely to snuggle in public, for example, like Danny and Carleen did. And Irene was not inspired to wear cutoffs that rode way up her butt, and neither did she snap her fingers to Herbert's guitar thumping and piano pounding, nor pop her gum in an irritating way while putting on her makeup. Irene liked Fred fine and it was about time she had a boyfriend, she figured, so they started dating. She took on Fred like a hobby, her own 4-H project. But on this escape trip to Seattle she was secretly glad to get away from him, too, at least for a spell.

Herbert's job on the ranch during hay season was doing the dishes, and he pitched in with the cooking some, too, or he might be sent to town for parts for the baler. The rest of the time he stayed in the family room playing the first few chords of "Purple Haze" on his beat-up guitar, over and over, or the more urgent intro to "Light My Fire" on the piano. He was pretty good, Viva said, and all self-taught. Sometimes he'd put Petula Clark on the stereo. "*Down*town!" Or the Temptations, singing smooth renditions, in their matching suits, of songs by Sly and the Family Stone. "Evuh ray *body* is a star-har..." Or Dionne Warwick, delivering a pop version of Aretha Franklin. "April fools! April fools! April fools! April fools!" Herbert would dance around the room, drumming a light tattoo on the coffee table, causing Melvin's face, on the rare occasions it wasn't out accompanying his body on the baler, to become even more impassive.

"Tell that April fool to waltz in here and set the table!" Herbert would poke Melvin's Best All-Around-Cowboy belt buckle with his two index fingers and then leap back as if it were red hot. When Herbert acted goofy Viva was happy.

~

After buying the sunglasses, Irene and Doreen wanted strangeness immediately, so they took the airport road out of Arboleda instead of Highway 2. The airport was one hangar and a wind sock out past the town dump. They meandered along county roads, part gravel and part paved, for most of the morning, trying to get back on the highway. This was okay, they decided, because for the moment it was themselves that they wanted to be full of, rather than any particular place. The goal mattered less than the fact that they were going.

Grasshoppers came zinging through the car windows. They listened to "Swap and Shop" on "cutey radio" KUTE. The Cow Belles were having a bake sale at that evening's jackpot roping. Next came the jingle for "Tip Top Toggery...of course!" Irene thought about the August tradition instituted by Viva of lining Irene and her sisters up in the basement store room to determine usable hand-me-downs for school clothes, and then making a list for the purchase of a few new things. That feel of wool on sun-browned limbs. Sweet, but uneasy, dreams of metamorphosis.

In September she would leave home. She would go to junior college at Crag Community College, CCC. She was going to get an Associate degree, work her way toward a teaching certificate. She'd stay with Dad's cousin Frank and his wife Mitzie, who had a room ready for her, and come back to the ranch on weekends. She viewed this plan as a stepping-stone to going to Seattle. She didn't want to go to Seattle just now, she had announced to Viva and Dad, who were secretly relieved, as the college funds were about all dried up from The Big Girls, even with the America's Promise, and who knew what Herbert might want to do? She would definitely, eventually, go to Seattle, Irene said. But not yet.

Soon after Doreen's arrival at the University of Washington three years previous, she was tear-gassed by the King County police in front of Suzzallo Library. Doreen and her sorority sisters sang soulful peace songs and may or may not have camped out overnight on the library steps with a whole lot of guys. They were new to dissent and they were loving it. They were radical pledges.

Viva circled the house and methodically watered the shrubs each evening that summer, the summer after Doreen's first year at college. Then she did it the next summer, after both the Big Girls officially had left home, though they were back again for the hay season. And she did it now, all through the summer that had begun with multiple splenectomies and was to conclude with Irene going to CCC. Viva watered the shrubs and the few geraniums and some other scrawny, unnamed flowers that managed to escape the wind. Those outdoor flowers barely had a chance. She planted geraniums because she said they were hardy. Irene and Herbert, when they were real little, used to pull off the soft petals to make blood.

Doreen and Carleen hoped to move to somewhere like San Francisco to get jobs and take time off from college. After a year of talking about it, Herbert was moving to town. Melvin was moving nowhere, he declared, though no one had asked.

Snap, Crackle, and Pop lay panting on the grass, watching Viva's every move. Most evenings Irene lay on the grass too, touching with her fingertips the rough ridge of the surgery scar on her stomach, thinking about her departure at the summer's end, shifting her position to keep near her mother, waiting for Fred, who got off work late at the Conoco, to come down the road in his pickup. She looked up at the first star and listened to the sad and monotonous sound of an airliner—heading out to Minneapolis, maybe—just the jet trail visible. She felt sick and giddy with the silent spinning toward change. Her mother's sprinkling, Irene liked to think, was an excuse to be out in the dusk, keeping quiet company with her youngest daughter. But she knew that Viva was preoccupied with thoughts of Doreen's strange delinquency (her hair looked like hay gone to mold!) and Carleen's fluctuating relationships (that girl dumped Danny every other week!). And she probably was thinking about Herbert, too, both strange and fluctuating, dancing all day in the family room instead of inventorying whatever household items he might need for his basement studio in town.

~

On the morning of the sunny sister car trip over back roads that felt as temporary and springy as boardwalks, Irene pushed away those anxious evenings in the yard. She and Doreen in their new sunglasses soared along the ridge line, along the wide-open grasslands where Indian kids on horses raced bareback, though only a few now, and only once in a while. She and her sister were wild, and they were wacky. The world enfolded them in perfectly-etched promise. They rushed to meet it—women warriors, warrior stars! They didn't know that they would wreck the Plymouth late at night on the floating bridge, just short of Seattle.

It would not be their fault. A drunk and confused Shriner, still dreaming of his mini-car performance in that morning's annual Seafair parade, would stop right in their lane. They would have no choice but to crash into him. He would reassemble himself at their window, bleeding from under his tasseled hat, and demand an explanation. His wife would glower magnificently behind him, wearing a ballooning cape. The night would whirl, and Irene would see whitecaps on Lake Washington.

Doreen would become near-hysterical with shocked laughing and then a huge, battered ship of a car would strike them from behind. The driver of that car, a woman with pale, hospital skin, would announce at the wrecking yard where the cars would be towed under Highway Patrol escort, that this time her husband really would kill her.

Herbert and Carleen would volunteer themselves to come on out on the bus to the rescue. They would be glad, themselves, to be rescued from the shameful pretext that they were helping with haying. There was nothing to be done; the car was totaled. And there they all were now, stranded in Seattle, sleeping on the floor at the

house of Darleen's old boyfriend. To get home they would borrow
their Seattle cousins' VW bus, which the cousins were looking to
sell, and on minor highways west of Whitefish (a meandering route
Herbert chose, to extend the reprieve), the four of them would jump
fully clothed into the Kootenai River—ostensibly to cool off, but
really in tribute to the wild and perspicacious humans they hoped
to become. Irene would slosh back out, carefully wringing out her
t-shirt, and pretend to laugh, trying not to cry.

Irene didn't know any of this as her hair haloed out in the car's
rush and she sent the red radio needle searching for stations from
Great Falls or from Canada, stations you could sometimes get on days
like this, wind-clean and empty except for that one, high jet, its voice
sporadically droning in the lulls. (*. . . there is nothing to be done . . . nothing to be done . . .*)

The radio signals came sailing down over acres and acres of
farmland, long strips of wheat and fallow that might look to the passengers in the jet like huge quilts lying over a deserted land, blankets
for giants or gods. A closer look might show combines or mowers
performing a slow crawl, driven by farm boys, or maybe custom cut-
ters, itinerant workers hired to help with the harvest. To the people
in the jets, the machines would look insect-sized, their work one of
unraveling. Robot locusts, methodically tearing, chewing, and spit-
ting out the grain.

~

The going, always the going, never quite arriving. That's what
she remembered. Shuffling along the waterfront every few years,
sniffing the unfamiliar air, feeling the strange mist, peering nervously up at the looming city, the noise of it like a rough surf and a
disconcerting reminder of eastern Montana's continuous wind. They
munched galvanized strips of fat-fried clams, bought bright replicas
of Japanese fishing floats, and became quarrelsome, at odds with each
other and embarrassed before their cousins.

Sometimes they stayed at a motel, if Dad and Melvin also came and there were too many of them to stay with the relatives. One spring they all played hooky from work and school and went to the Seattle World's Fair, where nine-year-old Herbert filmed long home movies of the padded vinyl next to the window of their monorail car. There are a few parts of the surviving reels with people, Irene's family, milling about like cows and calves at a crossing. The relatives stand still in the center and smile off in various directions, the soft, humming click of the movie projector the only sound.

Herbert was intrigued with the international exhibits more than the stuff about space exploration. He filmed many minutes of flamenco dancers at the World's Fair, a man and a woman silently spinning out a torturous courtship on stage, their bodies arched toward an eternal yearning, only their feet keeping them grounded and alive. The dancers seemed never to reach the place they were seeking, they seemed never to arrive. Eventually they flung themselves apart, twirled away from their frustration, and Irene and her siblings, watching the replay, breathed sighs of disappointment and relief.

~

Back in the car again. They are going to Seattle. They are going to the opera. Irene is again a little kid. Early summer. Doreen is haltingly reading aloud a synopsis of the opera, *Aida*. Viva's brother sent it to them, out of the blue, a very surprising thing to find in the mail box.

Aida's lover Radames has just been sentenced to be buried alive.

"Good Lord!" says Viva, as Doreen determinedly bends back the pages of the booklet, so it will stay open. Viva's brother took it into his head that Viva's children should see more city culture, and Doreen, Carleen, Irene, and Herbert were chosen for this second trip of the year, The Big Girls selected for opera attendance. Melvin, fresh from his first year of kindergarten, opted to stay home with Dad and help with the chores. The Big Girls and Viva are to accompany Viva's brother and Aunt Peggy to the Seattle Opera House and Irene and

Herbert are to stay with their cousins and a teenaged babysitter in the split-level house in the bleak suburb on the edge of the sparkling city.

Irene communicates with her cousins by way of odd feints toward sociability. One or another of the children picks up a toy or a puzzle or a game. The rest watch, waiting for a cue. The babysitter, though always on the phone, has made them shy with each other. Herbert does not pick up any toys, and he does not talk. At home he would be flinging the stuffed animals into the air, upsetting the Chinese checkers board. Irene slowly disengages his fingers from her arm, disconcerted by his silence.

She picks up a large marble that looks like a green glass eyeball and puts it in her pocket, holding it there in the palm of her hand. She thinks: *I have this marble here, in my pocket, in my hand, and I will have it there still later, when everyone's returned, and I will look back at the me of now with the eyes of then.*

When Viva left for the opera she was wearing a dress that showed a faint shadow between her breasts. Irene had never seen Viva wear such a dress. Viva was nervous; she fanned herself with a Kleenex and looked unhappy. The dress had been sewn especially for this occasion by Custom-Cut Fashions in Crag. It was patterned a deep red and a shimmering blue.

Through the window Irene sees in the distance an illuminated sky. She thinks about Aida and she thinks about the opera, picturing the stage, part castle, part grave. She rolls the smooth, cool marble in her palm. Dark pines drip and stir toward the house.

She can just barely hear the constant city sound.

17.

Fake Snowflakes
Alfred and Iris

On the day of the Seattle city bus crash, the day before the beginning of the RealRoutes Chartered Quests PARADISE PROMISE
SuperValue Tour to Amazing Asia!, in the late afternoon when the
cold rain stopped and the heavy, coastal clouds were laced with light,
Santa Claus came to town.

The town was a Seattle suburb where Alfred's second cousin
Joe lived. It used to be a small village some distance from the city,
discrete and separate, on the glassy waters of Puget Sound. Now it
was much the same, but there was no clear demarcation between
where it ended and where other urban entities began, and, through
no particular agency of its own, its simple facts had become selling
attributes, distinguishing markers in the print materials and spoken
language of the Chamber of Commerce, and the Uptown Association, and local realtors. It had "a small-town feel." It was "on the sparkling waters of Puget Sound."

The small town might once have seemed mostly gray and windy,
a bit lonely with the one movie marquee, and at the end of main street
that silvery mass of water stretching out with sparkling waves, or
maybe no visible movement at all. Kids might have walked down

this street and dreamed of their occasional visits to Seattle, a half-hour drive down the shoreline, through the rainforest, to a bright and busy place, the place they tapped into every day at 5 p.m. when they watched a kids' variety show on television. Teenagers might have driven their souped-up cars down this street beaten by rain, the houses working-class small (now "charming"), the front yards meager (now "quaint"), the shops, selling hardware and groceries (these days, scented candles and soapstone whales), closed by six. The teenagers, not realizing their own children someday would adopt leather pants, shaved heads, tattoos, and chains, in an effort to regain the grim reality once reposing in the pre-improved town, would have dreamed of the day when they could leave.

Yes, the town now was cute, some might say overly so. But Alfred's second cousin Joe and Joe's second wife Eunice had grown up near each other in the empty drylands of Wyoming. Their childhoods had been even sparer than this town's early years. So they were enthusiasts for latter-day charm. The water made them feel always on vacation, they said, at least that was its effect during their early years on the coast, just the two of them and baby Kevin. Also, they were glad to be out here far away from their former lives, those disastrous early marriages and Joe's unpromising prospects on the family ranch. He was a second son, so he could leave. He left.

He had first worked at a service station, then got a nice pot of cash when the river-bottom part of the ranch got sold. That, along with his disability ("bum knee"), and Eunice's job as a paraeducator at the elementary school, was enough to live on, plus they'd bought their little house back when Seattle was just Seattle, and this was just a house to live in, not a dream property in an up-and-coming locale.

The service stations now sold dark chocolate truffles and hazelnut steamers and the downtown mini-mall offered chair massages for tired shoppers. Joe and Eunice described these things to Alfred and Iris with barely-suppressed glee. (Their house was worth a fortune!) And there was a gas fire that flickered in a fake stone hearth at the center of nearby Pacific View Plaza, with crackling sounds issuing from a hidden speaker. And you could bet that was all-native, weathered wood on the rough-hewn benches, everything decorated with fiber "snow". As Joe described the Plaza's amenities, Iris pictured patrons roasting chestnuts at the mall, right there in the atrium.

The day of Santa's arrival, the day before Day 01 of their PARADISE PROMISE, Alfred and Iris watched a bit of the coverage of the bus accident, the driver shot, the bus sailing off the bridge. They sat eating Chex mix with Joe and Eunice and baby Kevin, now grown up. They were waiting for the local weather report, the men enjoying beers while their wives sipped wine. Alfred and Iris wanted to find out about the flying conditions.

"No earthquakes, let's hope, no bomb attacks, no storms at sea!" Joe emitted a rat-a-tat laugh.

Kevin cooked at a vegetarian restaurant called Tabula Rasa on Brooklyn Avenue in the University district, and he played in a band. He seemed to Alfred and Iris to be a friendly young man, despite the pierced eyebrows, the spider web tattoo in and around his left ear, and the little tuft of hair growing out of the cleft in his chin like lichen. He'd been over helping Joe do something or other to the engine of Eunice's car. Now he popped open a beer and said "Tropical Cyclone Sarika" –his amiable response to Iris's inquiry about the name of his music group.

"Cambodian drummer," he explained, when Alfred asked where he'd got a name like that. Eunice confessed that she always thought it sounded like something good to eat, a Dairy Queen treat! Kevin fished a 45 vinyl recording out of a crumpled plastic bag and handed it to Alfred. It was a couple of their songs, Kevin said, a demo. Alfred didn't know how he'd be able to listen to it without a turntable. He'd once had a turntable, but he took it to the city dump, oh, how long ago? Alfred turned to Iris. Iris wasn't quite sure. Kevin said, well, you can keep it anyway, and then he went back outside, and Eunice said he was the sweetest boy you would ever want to meet. Iris nodded.

Though his music was certainly not everyone's cup of tea. Eunice put her hand on Iris's arm in a gesture of confiding. A lot of screaming.

"Loud enough to bring down the world!" Joe laughed a rat-a-tat.

Their attention turned to the legs of the murdered bus driver and the legs of the murderer-turned-suicide, lying companionably together on the TV screen. Their bodies were mostly covered by a tarp, but the legs were exhibited for the camera so that the viewing audience would know that this really had happened, and that the KING-TV cameraman had been there to see.

"A holiday tragedy," said the anchorperson. "Motive unknown."

Then Joe and Eunice and Alfred and Iris set off to join the villagers for the post-Thanksgiving Friday night lighting of the giant Christmas star on the top of the Bon Marche at Pacific View Plaza, an annual tradition that signaled the official beginning of the Christmas shopping season, an event that Eunice said used to make Kevin jump up and down.

"O, star of Bon," Kevin said now, smiling in a sleepy way before wheeling out of the driveway on his big motorcycle without a helmet.

~

The brick approach to the Bon Marche was shiny and wet, as if it had been freshly washed. Children in new fleece hats trimmed with embroidery sat atop their fathers' shoulders or ate hot, gourmet popcorn from the trays of sleek, elongated strollers. The strollers, explained Joe, were specially designed for jogging.

"Or fleeing!" Joe jingled his car keys incessantly, a nervous habit, or maybe he meant to be festive. "Fleeing, ha ha ha! That's what Kevin would say."

There were far fewer children than adults. Children seemed scarce.

A shaky, accordion-playing comedian from the yesteryears of Seattle television laboriously ascended a set of portable steps to a temporary platform and told Scandinavian jokes, seemingly oblivious to the fact that Seattle's ethnic iconography had long ago abandoned tulips and clogs and gone Asian. Then he sang Christmas carols, which sounded like advertising jingles in his up-tempo interpretations. Eunice said that she used to count on this comedian's half-hour program on Channel 5 to keep Kevin occupied while she prepared dinner. Iris thought of studio laughter filling small houses surrounded by wind and rain. At the end of the street, that black, spangle-tipped water, moving slowly, like a sentient being, stirred by an incoming storm. Eunice said she would be sure to tell Kevin that the comedian had been here and that he was still alive.

The Christmas carols continued. They were carefully secular. "Jingle Bells," "Rudolph the Red-Nosed Reindeer," "Silver Bells." Everyone shivered in the damp. It was that dusk-descending moment, the time of day when, as a child, Alfred always had wanted to cancel plans for any overnight away from home. He had never let his pals know about that. He wished they would sing something religious right now, something with the Christ part of Christmas. He wished they'd sing "What Child is This?" He hummed it under his breath as cormorants winged in from Puget Sound, over the Plaza.

What child is this, who laid to rest . . . ?

He couldn't remember the words. He pulled Kevin's 45 out of his raincoat pocket and read the title of the song on side A, as if that might help. *God's Archipelago.* Interesting. The little record seemed so primitive, poignant, like something a kid might have. Why not a CD? Alfred finally had a CD player, having moved on from cassettes, but now he guessed it was back to records. He turned the record over to side B. *Death by Drowning.* He put it back in his pocket.

Keeping his eyes on the last thin glint of daylight in the sky, Alfred tried to think of some of the meaningful music he'd been exposed to since he'd joined the Schubert Club, a men's choir made up mostly of retirees, directed by a professor emeritus from the university. Alfred strove to have at least two hobbies or activities going in his life at all times, on the advice of *Prevention* magazine, and singing in groups was one of them. Iris had her book club and such. At one time, for her main activity, she had wanted to adopt a little baby, but he put the kibosh on that. A bad idea. Too damn many people already, he said. Iris pointed out that the little baby would have been born anyway. Born and then given up, maybe even killed or set out on a hillside, if a girl. So it's a wash, Alfred said. Anyway, it wouldn't look like you, he continued. And kids weren't a hobby, believe you me. His friend from high school, Harry, and Harry's wife whatsher-name, had adopted a little Asian baby and the school kids in their town called her Chink. They didn't mean any harm, those damn kids. They thought she was an Indian. But he and Iris with a little China doll? No thank you.

Alfred grew indoor orchids and belonged to a gun club and cor-responded with enthusiasts for each. He did that and the singing, and Iris had her phone conversations with her mother, and her book club. When the Schubert Club needed baritones, he'd switched to that from the church choir. The new director at the church choir had been too agitated or what do you call it? Hepped up. Wanting to throw out the old hymns, sing spirituals. Presbyterians doing that. Even Alfred knew there was nothing worse. The Schubert Club was a secular organization, but some of the texts were scripture-like, with musical arrangements by Ralph Vaughan Williams. *What is man, that Thou art mindful of him?* And so forth.

The gigantic Perkins American flag across the parking lot was starting to stir in a rising wind. Alfred tried to think of the words from a work the Schubert Club had been rehearsing every Tuesday night all fall in preparation for the winter concert. It was Vaughan Williams' *The Sea Symphony*, text by Walt Whitman.

Wherefore unsatisfied soul? Whither oh mocking life?

That's all he could bring up at the moment.

Iris said she enjoyed attending Alfred's Schubert Club concerts. Sometimes she even attended the rehearsals, sitting out in the darkened auditorium waiting to give Alfred a ride home. His night vision was going to hell. She said she was glad she didn't have to sit alone in church now, since Alfred had quit singing in the church choir and rejoined the regular congregation at the Sunday service. She had thought to participate in the church choir with him, once upon a time, but when she discussed it with Alfred, saying she wasn't sure she should do it because she wasn't a very good singer, Alfred had said: "Then don't."

The accordionist began a crazed-robot rendition of "Sleigh Bells." All eyes were on the sky, looking for the laser image of Santa that was promised to appear.

Wherefore unsatisfied soul? Whither oh mocking life? It seemed to Iris that Whitman posed plenty of questions. Sitting in the dark, waiting for Alfred, she felt that for the space of an hour and a half the questions were answered. She felt for awhile the embrace of life—*Behold! The sea, itself!*—the life she could see before her, anyway, life within the horizon, so neatly segmented into units of time: nine to five, Friday afternoon, day 01, 02, Tuesday nights.

Today, a rude, brief, recitative! Of ships! sailing the seas!

Alfred remembered more of the song now. He could picture the way the bold and portly soloist stretched out his arm, palm upraised.

"Fros...ty, the snowMAN!" The cluster of adults struck a jolly tempo for the small scattering of children. That was Kevin's favorite Christmas carol when he was little, Eunice told Iris, who nodded. Alfred, brought back to the holiday theme, hummed "Oh Come, Oh Come, Emmanuel."

O come, O come, Ema-a-a-new-el, to ransom captive I-i-is-raw-el...

He definitely was feeling a touch of pre-trip melancholia.

"A girlfriend might help," Eunice said to Iris, in reference to her fear that Kevin did not have a healthy lifestyle outside the restaurant.

"Oh yes," Iris said. Iris always listened to parenting concerns with an alert guardedness, searching hard for comparative anecdotes that didn't involve Tyke, her and Albert's aged springer spaniel.

"All journeys start with an anxious pang of doubt! You feel suddenly an orphan." Iris's mother quoted that to Alfred and Iris as she waved goodbye to them from her carport in Spokane, sending them off on their PARADISE PROMISE, which she'd fully underwritten and even insisted upon, saying *You* go because *I* can't. Hard of hearing and ailing, she once had been head librarian at Crag Community College, over in Montana, a career that made her prone to literary references. A quote about an orphan struck Alfred as odd for a send-off. She thumped her walker as an encouraging salute.

"It's Lawrence Durrell!" she exclaimed impatiently to Alfred, who never knew what she was talking about. *"Sicilian Carousel."*

A shiny, red fire engine bearing a thin, waving Santa eased between the old-fashioned lamp posts and down the faux-cobbled street. The laser light show had developed a glitch, the loud speaker reported, this real person approaching was the backup Santa. The accordionist whipped into "Here Comes Santa Claus," and somewhere beyond the periphery of the crowd's vision, but just within hearing, an ambulance and a police car wailed away, the mournful sounds receding like the backwash of a wave.

18.
Into the World

The man's face was delicate, with a high forehead. His body was compact, like Ron's, and he wore small, round glasses with tortoise-shell frames, his thinning blond hair swept neatly behind his ears. Cradling his glass of beer with the tips of his fingers, he spoke intently to his companion at their sidewalk table, a young woman with a muted, nondescript grace, a Caroline Kennedy appeal. Their words—English? German? Swedish?—were absorbed into the sounds of the humid night market and the sex shows all around.

Irene had her first bite of a long-awaited dinner, a bowl of noodles with squid. A slow-growing burn worked its way down her throat, an expanding cloud of peppery heat. The tourists scrutinizing the nearby stands loaded with t-shirts and sunglasses cast a few glances at her red, shiny face. Like her, they recently had marched—brisk and purposeful—past the open door to Pussy Galore. This street once had been a respite for soldiers on leave from jungle warfare. Now tourists populated the walks, while the sex trade inside the doors remained still active.

Irene bent low over her writing, wiping her eyes. She was pretending to make a list or to be writing a letter to someone, so that she did not seem strange.

She had left the group that day, opting for a side excursion with the Unitarians. They were going to a war memorial, while the PARADIS-ERS were going to the World Trade Center, an eight-story mega-mall (destined for a name change in a few years' time). Irene went in search of a bathroom and became separated from the Unitarians at the central bus station. They apparently forgot she had joined them, or perhaps thought that she had changed her mind, and she found herself swept up with a group boarding a bus headed to the coast. Her fellow passengers were local people, one and all, and when they spilled onto a small-sized ferry boat at the end of the bus trip, she did too. She was afraid to be left again, though she had no idea where she was going.

She still was shaken from this unplanned excursion, and exhausted. But exhilarated, too, at her new sense of connection with this country and its peoples. At various intervals during her day-long, roundtrip excursion she had handed over ticket money, the bills and coins counted out for her, some placed gently back into her palm. She had made it back to the center of the city by showing around her guidebook (which yielded no explanation of where, exactly, she was) and saying, "Hotel New Riverview" (too new to be listed, so eliciting no response even from the American college kids she found on the island where the ferry docked).

Now here she was, if not back at the hotel, at least somewhere with grown-up foreigners. She had made it back! Or at least to here, a tourist zone, where she was deposited by an exasperated tuk-tuk driver who gave up on finding her hotel. The tuk-tuk drivers had swarmed her upon her return to the central bus station, and she just arbitrarily picked one. What a mistake. He was barely thirteen, if a day. And he had to rev the engine mightily to even keep the thing going. She had been choking on the fumes when he finally decided to dump her. She was so relieved to finally find a bathroom! (Nothing you would want to write home about, though it undoubtedly would make its way into First Wednesday conversations.) And now here she was, alive, initiated, and intact!

She jotted down notes for her potential article for the *Arboleda Pioneer*. She was thinking it might become a mini-meditation on travel in the current world.

I like to be going somewhere, more than being anywhere.

That seemed good. (This writer, dear reader, is intrepid!)

I like the tickets, the timetables, the seat assignments. Being on the road, for me, is being in line. Ready to board. I like to be among the world's departures.

That last didn't sound quite right. She gulped a big beer in between sentences. She nibbled the fiery noodles, too, because she was starving after all that traveling. Then she had to gulp some more beer, quickly, trying to drown the fire before it could spread. Scribble notes, gulp beer. Nibble noodles, gulp beer.

Sitting on beaches is nice. For an hour or so. Irene hastily signaled for another big beer and searched the bottom of her nylon bag for a Kleenex.

But I'd rather be in transit than in paradise.

Her tears were becoming the real tears of a person who was getting more than halfway looped, alone, sleep-deprived, and filled with the standard traveler's feelings of longing and loss. But she was filled with a sharp prescience, as well, the kind that causes one to fixate with ill-defined awe and total mesmerism on someone else's face—that man with the thinning blond hair—awe and mesmerism not felt by Irene since her very first date with Fred, her very first sips of beer, bumping along on hot prairie tracks, glancing not sideways at Fred, but forward to the front seat at Danny's fair hair, just brushing his collar. Fred's brother Danny, at the wheel, Carleen nipping his ear.

I didn't go to the island in order to get there.

She felt an epiphany coming on. (That was a good word, sort of prickly and popping. The Feast of the Epiphany! Something to celebrate.)

I went there because it was somewhere to go.

Yes, the night was popping. (The *Pioneer* editor didn't need to know it was all a crazy mistake.)

I like having a destination.

The night was prickly! (She blew her nose.)

But no itinerary.

He was a teacher, that man with the classic, graceful woman. He was a published poet, a well-known writer. Or . . . he was a salesman, a dentist, a computer programmer. This country was a bargain right now, she'd heard. He is just like you, she told herself, scowling at a family of four eyeing her table. Another tourist.

Maybe so, she answered herself. But being here makes him shine, obviously. (She started a whole new page in her notebook.)

This man is transformed from his ordinary life, and his double is . . . illuminated! He is this mesmerizing self.

The man glanced at her. (Were her lips moving?) Irene bent closer to her writing.

I crossed the strait in a toy-colored boat.

It still seemed heroic.

Islanders were returning from market on the mainland, baskets of silver sea-somethings at their feet.

She made a stab at some travelogue language. She glanced at the man and saw that he was laughing, his eyes were crinkled closed. She began laughing too. She began writing for the man. She began writing to him. She would tell him about her day.

On the island, a parade of lone backpackers was in constant motion. Young. They wore that pinched traveler's face—focusing on the horizon, feigning distraction.

"This is just a chance happening." That's what they wanted their faces to say. *"This slogging through warm, white sand next to a deep, blue sea. I am actually on my way to somewhere else: Malaysia, graduate school, the pier for the next ferry out."*

The appealing young woman pushed back her chair. The mesmerizing man finished his beer. Irene wrote faster.

On the island, I felt full of myself. But only myself. I felt aware of being single. I mean to say . . . my singularity. On the boat, though, this feeling gave way to . . . She searched for a word and gave up. Her next words were only felt, her pen on pause.

(There is an intimacy to being anonymous in a small, unstable space.)

When the woman touched his arm, the man's contained look of pure pleasure spilled over into a crooked smile. Irene remembered now what it was she wanted to say about her day trip, about travel in general. She sat up straight and gripped her pen.

Ferry boats sink all the time.

The boat that day had, in fact, been listing to one side and drawing water.

They carry a whiff of disaster. (She had never been on a ferry boat before, but the *Pioneer* editor didn't need to know that.)

This potential, I feel, binds us together.

She lapsed back into her reverie.

(Sadly, it is at the point of arrival that our camaraderie evaporates, as we waft out into the world.)

The man and the woman pushed back their chairs and stood. Irene looked at them over her beer glass as she enjoyed a last, long drink. Then she bowed her head to her notebook.

I raised my face to the late-afternoon light. The ferry chugged along. We clung to each other through tension, if nothing else, like droplets in the sea.

The waiter brought her bill.

When we hit the shore, we scattered.

She looked up and they were gone.

19.
Body Splash

"¡Olé! ¡Olé!"

The group stared as Ron gyrated at the front of the boat, singing some form of Spanish and attempting the moves of a flamenco dancer. A small amplifier lay near his feet and he clutched a black microphone, his voice dropping to a mutter as he rapidly scanned a pink song sheet, his mirrored sunglasses flashing in the setting sun.

"No matter. No problem. My happy heart sings!" He broke into English with a grin. "All lovely, so lovely. It give-ah me wings!"

"Thank you, thank you, yes, okay! Haha! ¡Olé! ¡Olé!"

Ron slammed the microphone onto its stand and rushed to the back of the boat. His job for this increment of the evening was over. He had shown them how it was done.

Special entertainment had been promised for the second and final dinner cruise and this was it. The lists of possible song choices and their lyrics fluttered like large flower petals in the hands of the passengers, who were clustered around tables on the sheltered open deck. Ron had demonstrated how to punch in a song number on the little amplifier, just as on a juke box—a "nifty trick," in Keith's language, a "palliative surprise," in Mr. Small's, who confessed he had been dreading the special entertainment, certain it would be ethnic as hell. Keith looked at him questioningly. He thought that Mr. Small was keen on culture, the traditional traditions. Oh sure, traditional culture, Mr. Small said, you betcha, everything's full of it, chock-a-*block*, it is all so "ethnic." He turned and wiggled his two index fingers at Mrs. Small, who said Whadijya expect? Mr. Small got this way at this general point on all their travel adventures. Ready to go home to the tea shop. Ethnic-speshnic, said Pete, his statement directed toward the river bank. The cruise boat plowed along through the roiling brown water, the sky matching the color of the song lists, the diners' cheeks adding to the general rosy hue.

A small child ran along the river's edge and waved to the boat with both arms, shouting "Hallo!" then doubling over with glee.

"There is always someone at the bottom," said the elderly man with the bullet bolo tie. He was speaking to Denise, who was lightly drumming on their table with both hands, her eyes on the back of the boat where the buffet was assembling. The man hadn't managed to achieve a first name basis with anyone. She of the beaded bracelets, his usual target, wasn't on the boat today. Pooped out, he guessed. Couldn't take the pace.

"Someone's gotta be at the bottom of the heap."

This was a discourse, of sorts, on social Darwinism. All the dinner cruisers, as they filed up the gangplank to board the boat, had looked down upon a solo man in a needle-nosed canoe who was preparing a delicious-looking bowl of vegetables for himself, ladling the aromatic mixture out of a bamboo steamer into a bowl of broth and noodles. Remembering the buffet associated with the week's previous pleasure cruise (a leisurely route close to shore that allowed those on board to spy on people in their modest homes), they'd hoped he might be selling those bowls of food. But this did not seem to be the case. He carefully consumed his dinner as they all looked on.

Possibly because of his tattered t-shirt, and ignoring the quality of his cuisine compared to the curdled, ill-defined glop served from tepid chafing dishes on their other dinner cruise, they'd decided that the man was poor, which sparked some general self-examination on the part of the PARADISERS, as they quaffed complimentary Heinekens.

"This buffet could feed a village for a week," asserted Irene, her voice sounding oddly high to her ears. (*A week, a week . . .* came the echo.) "I don't mean the Native Village, I mean a village village!" She attempted a playful punch on Pete's arm.

She had purchased more postcards featuring Hill Tribe children "in their skivvies" (Pete's comment when she passed them around), and she'd memorized captions that struck her as useful bits of information. The Hill Tribe children were assimilating into the mainstream while retaining their unique culture, Irene related, her face instantly serious. She was glad that Denise was sitting at a different table. Whenever Irene shared interesting Hill Tribe information, the look on Denise's face made her wish she hadn't.

"Some . . . day."

Keith, who, at Ron's urging, had commandeered the microphone, was only on his second Heineken, a few beers behind some of the others.

"All my troubles fly so far . . . away."

He didn't usually drink beer and it seemed to be going straight to his head.

"But I need, I need, some-*one* to pay."

He was experiencing trouble reading the lyrics, having lost his glasses. The group was disconcerted to see Keith wipe his nose with the back of his hand and rapidly blink his eyes. Mrs. Small began clapping enthusiastically while simultaneously gesturing him toward his seat.

"Suddenly." He was determined to continue.

"I'm not HALF of what I ought to be." His voice swooped upward unexpectedly.

"Now I need . . . I need . . . today!"

Keith sat down, looking dazed, Mrs. Small solely appreciative. A small disturbance had broken out at the back of the boat, drawing the attention of everyone else. Denise, plate in hand, was challenging a German tourist from a separate contingent, all wearing name tags that said WELTMEISTERIN REISEBÜRO. She seemed to be challenging him to a fight. Denise, in fact, had struck a blow. The tourist, an attractive, fortyish man sporting a spiky haircut, was holding his right eye and swearing, in English.

"*God*. Dammit!"

"You take your place in line, asshole," Denise muttered. Her eyes were so smudged with mascara it looked as though she herself had been hit.

"I only backhanded him," she explained to Iris, next in line, whose face was frozen into a look of uncomprehending acceptance. Alfred remained at their table. In a gesture of defiance, he had said he wanted to wait a bit before eating.

"It's singing! Singing! We are singing now, everybody, yup!" Ron waved his napkin toward the front of the boat, nudging the German into a chair, away from Denise, who calmly filled her plate. Ron then leaned down and said something into the man's ear, jerking his head toward the entire PARADISE PROMISE group. The man made a rude gesture, and Ron demurred with his hands, as if the man were offering him an extravagant present. Then he planted himself in front of the German table, legs spread, arms folded.

Alfred now had the microphone and was smiling woodenly and tipping an imaginary hat. This performance was even more surprising than Keith's and equally unintelligible. Alfred, who was either somewhat reserved or prone to sulking, hadn't said much to the group the entire trip, beyond discussions of eggs in the morning. The miniature juke box was rasping out the accompaniment to "Roll Over Beethoven" but Alfred seemed to be singing some kind of doggerel with a yodeling refrain. The effect was discordant—rhythmically, melodically, and every other way imaginable.

Iris, having regained her seat, looked on, profoundly expressionless. In the most private recesses of her heart she simply was relieved that the evening's culture event was not folkloric. Alfred had shown an embarrassing proclivity to paw, in a way not at all fatherly, any young girl who looked folkloric, telling her, Iris, to take a picture. It was so out of character for him that Iris felt no anger at all, just a kind of pity and marital melancholy. But she wished he wouldn't do it, a sentiment reflected in the girls' faces.

During the course of Alfred's song Pete's cheeks had become increasingly red, and he was wheezing a great deal, his chest jerking convulsively. Mrs. Small sat with her elbows on the table, one hand over her mouth in a meditative pose, the other on Pete's arm, which she occasionally patted. Irene leaned forward to see if Pete was having a heart attack, but noted that he was in fact crying—crying?—no, giggling, and with a very peculiar, small animal sound, as he blew his nose with a napkin. Irene guessed they were all getting a little batty from bad sleeps. Finally, he pushed back his chair, grabbed his crutch, and lurched to the back of the gently swaying boat. Mr. Small kept dreamy time with his water glass and a spoon, tracing idiosyncratic rhythmic patterns in the air with a lacy fan that Mrs. Small had bought at a roadside stall.

"Yodelay hee hoo!"

Alfred didn't seem to be able to stop or proceed, and he began to look mildly terrified, although he did have a robust singing voice. His t-shirt was riding up, revealing a white strip of stomach rolling over his belt, and Iris saw that his fly zipper was not quite secured. Mrs. Small applauded vigorously and then hooted encouragingly as Alfred finally lumbered to his seat.

Pete stood clutching the boat railing and gazed back at all the goings-on. He was drinking another Heineken, having swiped a spare off the German table. They struck him, these people, as both ridiculous and brave. *Brave to be singing! Up in front of everyone like that. They sound so awful! Are they hearing some other music in their heads?* The little juke box seemed to have them in its grip (except Alfred). *No live piano player, just that little box!*

They were ordinary, these people, ordinary like him, but alien, too, apart from him. *It's like watching a movie.* They seemed trapped, and aging, and vulnerable, and . . . *lost* . . . *disabled* . . . His traveling companions seemed to Pete like delegates from a group home, when viewed at a slight remove.

Denise's assault victim stood on his chair and sang something in German in a loud, raucous voice, his beer bottle marking time, his pelvis rocking. He was mocking the PARADISE group, without a doubt, and the entire WELTMEISTERIN REISEBÜRO contingent—a collection of intellectual entrepreneurs herded about by two competent sisters—was laughing. A man with John Lennon glasses and a thin ponytail inhaled beer up his nose and stood abruptly, nearly knocking over his chair.

"Duh duh duh duh da duh da duh duh," now the German played an imaginary bass and attempted to sing a song by the Doors without benefit of accompaniment. His song never progressed beyond vague vocables, which were further obscured by laughter and shrieking, as the pink lyric sheets fluttered off the tables, blown by a gust of wind. It had begun to rain, the drops coming in sharp pellets

Mrs. Small, ignoring the elements, decided to take things in hand and perform a song from her Ms. UC Boulder days, when she was at her prime in so many ways. Clutching her fluttering, silk-like shawl around her throat, as raindrops hammered the protective awning, she smiled tenderly at the amplifier, and sang in a nicely-controlled alto, husky and rich.

"When I was a winsome lass . . . ."

She wondered if this song would be appropriate for the group at hand. It wasn't her winning Ms. UC Boulder number, but rather an off-color variation sung after the competition, when all the contestants had become sweetly shit-faced.

(Note: Although she won the Ms. UC Boulder talent competition and was besieged by love-struck environmental science majors for months, Mrs. Small by then had her heart set on Mr. Small—whom she'd met the previous summer when his outdoorsy sister inveigled her to go rafting through the Grand Canyon and Mrs. Small had to perform a vigorous procedure on Mr. Small after a nasty, soaking accident.)

". . . with a lissome ass . . ."

She was vamping, shamelessly.

Denise thumped her chair around so that her back was to the performance. *Make every year count! Keep your friggin' future wide open!* (Denise's mother was totally gone on motivational seminars.) She stretched her legs out straight and tilted her head to drink, raising the bottom of her 7-up can high. *Review your options!* She hated Heineken; she thought it tasted skunky.

"I'd win some and lose some..."

Keith, delegated to go ask Ron about the boat's happy-room facilities, paused in his inquiry to listen to Mrs. Small, putting his hand on Ron's arm momentarily for ballast. Irene reached for her reading glasses on their neon green stretchy cord and began scanning the song choices, smoothing her own flapping shawl away from her face.

"...and the rest is kinda crass."

Mrs. Small gave a full-throated chuckle and curtsied demurely.

The wind picked up, causing the boat to rock and water to splash up onto the deck. The pleasure cruisers emitted a group "ohhh!" and lifted their feet a few inches off the floor. The Germans shouted uproariously as a basket of rolls bounced off the buffet table. Pink song sheets lifted into the sky all at once, like a flock of rare birds, a magician's trick.

Pete turned away and leaned over the railing of the boat, contemplating the churning froth of the wake. Undulating her shoulders, Mrs. Small let her silk/polyester shawl slip down her bare arms, and Mr. Small moaned theatrically, causing everyone to laugh.

Irene next took her place at the microphone, amid applause for Mrs. Small. No one heard the splash.

20.

Bound Away

Their last meal was the Basic Breakfast at 3 a.m. The lone bus idled in front of the hotel, its luggage compartment open, a light rain diluting the fumes. The hotel lobby was darkened, and the dining area was silent. The Christmas carols began promptly at 7 a.m., but Alfred and Iris, Mr. and Mrs. Small, Irene, Denise, Keith, and all the rest would be gone by then, already up in the brilliant thin air, flying home, PARADISE left, "Amazing Asia!" evolving into a string of anecdotes involving big Buddhas, terrific ruins, food, taxicabs, and shopping.

Ron would say "My name is R-O-N" to another group of travelers, all new, just as he had every third morning of the week, processing the groups through in an over-lapping schedule of greeting, touring, napping, eating, and entertainment.

The lavish breakfast buffet was not yet in evidence—the round, tiered serving tables were shrouded by heavy cloths, the heating lamps turned off, the many chafing dishes empty and cold. It was cereal, juice, and plain doughnuts for all, but rumors circulated that a real breakfast would be served on the plane.

The conversation was quiet. Everyone was a little stunned to be up so early, or, in some cases, awake so late. The unifying theme was the amount of sleep everyone did or did not get prior to this dark departure for the airport.

Keith slept six hours. He took 3 mg of melatonin at 8 p.m., following the advice of a friend from back home, a gal at the RealRoutes agency who flew internationally several times a year. Keith's patch of hair was more askew than usual, and his hand demonstrated its customary tremor as he spooned sugar into his coffee, but he otherwise appeared rested and ready to go. His characteristic nervous feints toward engagement had been replaced by a peaceful look of accomplishment. He had found his glasses. Breath mints and light snacks were tucked up in a mesh drawstring sack secured in the side pocket of his ergonomically-aligned carry-on bag. His next trip was already scheduled, a ValueTour World Traveler Bonus Trip featuring SCANDINAVIAN DREAMS—Amazing Holland! He expected to photograph windmills and possibly tulips. He already had printed out some of the photos taken on the present trip at the 24-hour FotoShop near the hotel. (Yesterday at breakfast he showed everyone images of the ice sculpture swan on the breakfast buffet, even as they all paced before it.) Keith was looking forward to the flight back. He enjoyed being in such close proximity to other people contained in the moment and knowing just what he was supposed to do.

Irene slept barely three hours, but they were three hours straight in a row, which represented a better night's sleep than she'd enjoyed throughout the trip. She did not have to lob pillows at Denise's snoring head was why. Denise wasn't there. Which was also why Irene got such a late start on sleeping at all. Her own head didn't make contact with any pillow until nearly eleven, because she had been waiting up for Denise, who had gone to the hotel bar. (Although Lord knows, Denise had not felt compelled to wait up for *her*, or even inquire as to her absence, when she'd come home late from her solo noodle repast and the big beers.) At ten-thirty Denise came to the room to get Irene's room key card. Hers was long lost, and she was heading out to see a boxing match with "the German dude" from the boat. A boxing match! With all the culture this place had to offer. Irene couldn't resist commenting. Denise said that it was plain fists, no gloves, and she planned to sit in the front row and become anointed with blood. A perfect place to "assess her options and come to some decisions."

What a strange girl. Erratic, in Irene's view. She should take more of the St. John's Wort, or whichever. Just as Irene was going down to breakfast, Denise returned, not particularly blood-spattered, thank goodness. Now she was up there showering. The bus would leave at 4 a.m. no matter what. Ron said so.

Irene couldn't get too angry at Denise. She was still feeling a glow from her dinner cruise performance of the previous evening. She had marched straight up there to the microphone, punched the right number into the little boom box, closed her eyes and put her heart and soul right into it. "Here, There, and Everywhere" was one of Herbert's favorite car songs, you could almost hear him singing it, his lovely tenor adding harmony.

Herbert, Herbert, Herbert. He'd certainly helped her out with that song. People stopped eating! Heinekens were put on pause, mid-sip. She smiled as she thought of it. Well, she had done some singing in her day. Keith, standing next to Ron, stared at her as if star-struck! Even Ron made his mouth into a little "o" and widened his eyes. Mrs. Small clasped her hands and snuggled up next to Mr. Small, who patted her head lightly at the beginning of each phrase, stroking her hair with each pat, Alfred and Iris watching as if this were a tutorial.

Well, her voice was, after all, still fine. She was glad she had been able to finish the song, give everyone some pleasure and enjoy a little applause and even begin her next selection, "Bridge Over Troubled Water" before being completely interrupted by Pete. Good Lord! That certainly put the evening on its ear.

If Keith hadn't turned around, if he hadn't turned his back to the stage at just that moment, if he hadn't turned his face away from Irene to cover a bit of emotion, Pete's descent into the water might have gone unnoticed. Irene kept her eyes on Keith's back as she sang in her best, well-supported intonation the line with the silver bird, sailing on . . . And then—Good Lord! –over the rail of the boat Keith went, just flinging his whole creaky body right up and over, like he was doing the high jump!

"Man overboard!" Keith shouted, his call ending in a splash.

Then Ron stepped neatly over the railing and stood there for just a split second, staring at the water through his sunglasses and smoothing back his hair. And then *he* was gone. Fully clothed, both of them. Ron with that nice watch.

Irene's mouth remained open, but no sound issued forth. The little black amplifier continued on, impervious. People began jumping out of their seats and rushing to the back of the boat, which then began a see-sawing motion, like that ride at the State Fair, what was it? Pirates of the Caribbean.

Irene experienced some difficulty trying to get the microphone back into its stand, and of course everyone was shouting and scrambling about by then, so no help was to be had. The accompaniment continued to emanate from the little black box, the string sections soaring. Several chairs fell over. Irene fumbled with the knobs on the box, but couldn't get it to turn off. She could see that the tall German Denise had smacked was ripping at his shirt and kicking off his shoes, apparently intending to join in the rescue. Denise was near him, peering over the railing with interest. Mrs. Small yelled "Stop the boat, stop the boat," in every direction, since no one knew where the engines might be located or who on earth might even be piloting. The elderly man with the bullet bolo tie put on his glasses and proceeded to read all the instructions for unraveling the cord to a toy-sized Styrofoam flotation device that was affixed to the wall of the boat's shelter next to a rust-streaked fire extinguisher.

Mr. Small took the microphone from Irene's hand and lay it carefully on the portable amp.

"Take a bow, Madame Butterfly," he said, apparently unmoved by all the commotion. He was perhaps a little bit smashed. "The song is ended." Then he became rather kind, almost fatherly, saying "Come along, now" in his benign, sweater-vested manner.

"You go, girl," he added, patting her shoulder awkwardly.

Yes, she did have a fine voice. She had experienced a childhood full of song, the very best preparation one could possibly have, and then there had been her courses at CCC, then her sporadic career as a voice teacher, more so after Fred passed away, very satisfying, the teaching that is, although the money wasn't good, not enough to live on, just a little extra income to add to the monthly check Melvin gave her. Good thing she had her little house, and Fred left some cash, though not much, cash and a pickup truck, not the ice fishing truck, a different one, parked there out on the ranch for who knew how long in the old sheep shed. Enough, after she finally sold it, for a trip, so she finally bit the bullet, weary of the small town life, the winters, just one or two requested performances each year at community events, the Rotarian banquet, the Cow Belles pancake supper, the Second Thursday Wedding Season Fashion Preview, that sort of thing, the Elk's Club's annual Toast 'n Roast at the Red Lobster in Crag, which could be terrifying, those banquets. She didn't sleep for a week, but there might be a small stipend, or at least a free meal, which gave her occasion to sit down with people she might not sit down with otherwise, at least not regularly, well, as a matter of fact, that's how she came to be invited to participate in the First Wednesdays and the Second Thursdays in the first place, truth to tell. Without her voice she would have no friends at all.

She still did her vocal exercises most mornings, singing "me-me-me-me-me-me-me-me-meeee" up and down the scales.

~

Pete was clutching Sterling, somewhat ineptly. He had Sterling by a leg, in fact, upside down. He didn't want any breakfast, and he was going to stand, Pete said, because they were going to be sitting for seventeen goddamn hours. He didn't offer a sleep report. Keith—with whom Pete had managed to endure a tenuous roommate relationship that began well enough, then worsened, then, as the tour's end approached, improved—reported quietly that Pete spent the early morning hours outside on the balcony, smoking. He left the sliding glass door open, which made their room very warm and muggy, which Keith liked, because it reminded him of Africa. Keith woke to hear the creak of the crutch. Then he drifted back into a Fujicolor sleep full of water and song. (Melatonin, he'd been forewarned by Nancy from RealRoutes, could produce marvelous dreams.) He slept comfortably, Keith reported, glad to know that Pete was keeping watch.

No one was sure why Mr. and Mrs. Small chose to bestow Sterling upon Pete. Some of the group actually had been disposed to take on the bear, but the Smalls didn't ask around. The care of the bear had a term limit of ten days; their time was up, Pete was it. This undoubtedly had to do with the boat mishap and the subsequent tedium of Outpatients at the Catholic hospital. The Smalls felt an urge to give Pete something. Sterling was it.

The Smalls seemed to realize that Pete quite likely would not keep company with Sterling for the requisite ten days, but they said he could achieve a hand-off at some secondary airport in the hinterlands, thus adding to the overall interest of Sterling's trip. The Smalls seemed to know that Pete might not be invested in this project, especially, so they were careful to point out the pre-addressed cards concealed in the pocket of the bear's vest: Mrs. Dickinson's Fourth Grade Class, Arboleda Elementary School, Arboleda, Montana, 59429, USA, Planet Earth, the Solar System, the Universe, c/o God.

(Note: Irene—who had no idea Sterling was from Arboleda, because the Smalls never thought to mention it, and she hadn't visited with them as much as she had wanted to, so did not have occasion to divulge the name of her hometown, she just said "Crag," anyway, if anyone asked, Crag being more prominent on the map—was in for a surprise and a certain degree of pleasure, seeing her own self in the *Arboleda Pioneer* upon her return, standing with the PARADISE group around the bear in a photo sent to the paper courtesy of the Smalls.

The article, she would discover, was all about Sterling, and she wasn't identified, and no one recognized her, including Melvin on the ranch, or Dad and his cronies at Pleasant View, who couldn't be expected to anyway. And even though the *Pioneer* editor would respond to her inquiry about writing a short article about an interesting trip to Asia by saying that they already recently had run an article featuring Asia, compliments of Sterling and his friends—"but maybe next time"—she would still be pleased, and she would cut the photo out of the newspaper and attach it to her refrigerator with an elf magnet.)

Iris reported to Irene, when Irene inquired, that she had slept fitfully the night before. Did you dream? Irene asked. No, Iris answered. But, in fact, she did have several dreams. First, she dreamt that she was on a swaying platform and was screaming at Alfred. She was screaming "You don't hear me!" The platform turned into her kitchen table back home, and she was sitting at it feeling a confusion of things, unable to bring her traveling self neatly through the door. Iris still carried the wobbly feeling of sorrow and surprise that had emerged several seconds after she awoke from this dream. She hadn't known she was feeling unheard, especially. She and Alfred talked little, what was there to hear? When she went back to sleep, she dreamt she was singing, very loudly, to an appreciative audience, a catchy number by the Rolling Stones.

When pressed to give a sleep report, Monica of the beaded bracelets estimated that she got four hours. She was used to delivering such a report. She had been issued a single room at the trip's outset—a more expensive option—and the others had wanted to know, on a daily basis, if it was worth it.

Before going to sleep, Monica had a facial. She'd been feeling all wound up from rushing around soaking up last drops of experience. And she'd been feeling quite furious, still, that she had missed the whole episode on the boat, opting instead to go "adventuring," as she'd cagily called what had turned out to be an exhausting half-day tour of a hot sauce factory. The promised entertainment of the trip's previous boat excursion had been dismal. Young men in loin cloths beating gongs. Trying not to laugh, most of them. Tiki torches. An inexplicable pageant involving a ratty-looking tiger suit. Just whom did they think they were entertaining?

She sat on her bed and flipped through the booklet about the hotel's amenities, feeling sorry that the trip was over. It seemed that it had been just yesterday that they had arrived. The trip never had taken off, not really. She hadn't done a lot of the things she had wanted to do. She hadn't had a chance to try the local iced tea, for instance. Apparently, there was something really special about the local iced tea and she had missed it.

Monica had never had a facial in her life. She equated such things with idle housewives, country club matrons. But she punched the extension number and within twenty minutes was reclining in a comfortable chair and allowing the skin on her forehead, cheek-bones, and throat to be gently massaged in quick, circular motions by the small fingers of a young girl who used minty lotion and did not speak. The girl placed a warm, moist towel on Monica's face and a heavy, cotton blanket over her body, and slowly massaged her feet, even though Monica hadn't asked her to. Monica was surprised to discover that this careful attention to her body was making her cry. Fortunately, the towel absorbed her tears.

She thought about a Buddha they had seen on the tour. It had been the Buddha before the really big Buddha (which had been a reclining Buddha that certainly had impressed them all with its immense languor). The Buddha before the reclining Buddha also had been of giant proportions, so huge that a man could sit comfortably in the palm of the Buddha's hand. And a man had, in fact, been sitting inside the Buddha's hand. He sat cross-legged, barefoot and shirtless, casting out silky bolts of cloth of various colors. The cloth shimmered down into the waiting arms of another shirtless man who was stand-ing below, near the Buddha's toes. The two half-naked men carefully wrapped the Buddha in streamers of silk. Monica thought she ought to know why they did that, but she didn't. Outside the temple a very small Buddha quivered with bits of gold leaf that could be purchased at a table nearby and pressed to the stone. The flaky bits of gold haphazardly covering the Buddha looked like shiny skin. It looked regal from a distance, but, up close, decayed or diseased. And eerily alive.

A radio played in the hotel salon while Monica had her facial, the girl's fingers lightly tapping her cheekbones. The radio seemed to be broadcasting a talk show. The announcer and all the callers sounded both quarrelsome and pleased.

III.

21.
Limbo

Day 10. You will transfer from hotel to airport for your flight this morning on board Oceania Airways' spacious jetliner, homeward bound.

Ron arrived to escort them to the airport and send them on their way. He looked tired. His name tag was not quite evenly positioned. The previous evening Keith came upon him in the men's room off the hotel lobby speaking rapidly and angrily into his cell phone. When Ron saw Keith, he brought the conversation to a close and snapped the phone shut. There was a moment of silence.

"My child," he said, indicating his phone wearily. Then he clicked back to being Ron.

"Child of Gawd!" he broke into a smile. "Also 'kid,' right?"

Now, in the chilled, early morning hotel lobby, he was half singing, in a sleepy way, "We are together, together, together…"

This was something Ron had been doing at odd intervals for a day or so. At first the songs were identifiable Broadway show tunes.

"Little bird, little bird," Ron might chirp, waving them onto the bus. "In the sycamore tree…" But now the songs had become diffuse; their near-melodies sounded familiar, but they were not quite placeable. Perhaps he had run through his repertoire, Mr. Small speculated. Perhaps he had run out of things to say, Mrs. Small offered. Perhaps he was on something, Mr. Small countered. Mrs. Small yawned.

"Goodbye, goodbye..." Ron switched to a new vague tune.

Ron deflected all discussion and speculation regarding Pete's accident (or his attempt, depending on who was talking). He acknowledged the fall (or jump) off the boat with an appropriately serious expression. But as to the heroic behavior of Keith and himself, he offered no comment.

After Mrs. Small finally found the captain, the very same man who had been eating that delicious-looking bowl of noodles and greens, the boat circled back toward the close-knit clump of splashing bodies, and the lanky German bounced the extricated lifesaver off the head of one of them. There was a graceless rescue (pushing and pulling up a small ladder), an emergency docking, and then a taxi ride to the nearest hospital, Sisters of the Sacred Heart, and a long wait at Outpatients for Ron and Keith and Pete. Ron was happy that Pete—who no, did not swim, and yes, had swallowed some water— was fully recovered. Ron was sure that Pete would rest comfortably on the return flight.

Pete shrugged. Pete wasn't talking.

"Comfortable, sure, you bet." And then Ron laughed off all further inquiry and seemed to suffer a momentary loss of English. Taking his cue, Keith was behaving exactly the same way as Ron. They were co-conspirators, Ron and Keith. They had Pete's back. They were in it together. Keith beamed at Ron and kept his lips sealed.

"We are waiting, waiting, waiting," Ron crooned, swing his collapsed umbrella like a pendulum. "We are waiting for the world..."

He concluded this farewell riff with "Okay!" and a satisfied chuckle before briefing the group about security measures at the airport.

"They will light you up!" he promised.

"X-ray the bags," explained Mr. Small, when Irene looked worried. "Scanners, regular stuff. Routine." Irene sneezed daintily. Ever since the boat she had been feeling just a touch of a cold coming on. Mr. Small had put in a special request for orange juice for Irene at the Basic Breakfast. Only apple and pineapple juice had been readily available, so he'd made his way into the kitchen area and found a bus boy sleeping there, and the boy had rustled up some orange juice at Mr. Small's request. Irene extracted a Kleenex now from a little plastic packet with a flower design and foreign script. She confided to the group that she was looking forward to getting back to the part of the world where there's always a Safeway.

"Once you get home you will try to go away from home again!" Ron delivered a final, admonishing aphorism as they all headed for the bus.

And then they were gliding toward the airport (gliding...gliding...). Everyone was quiet in the plush seats. They rode ten feet above the earth, the windows steamy and streaked. Some of the group had fallen asleep again, some looked down on the sparse 4 a.m. traffic that flowed in sporadic waves down the wet thoroughfare, the motorcycles, the taxicabs and buses, the private cars, the tuk-tuks, the trucks. They caught glimpses here and there of people they would never know, early risers waiting at bus stops, workers wearing bamboo hats and face masks who swept the edge of the roadway with stiff brooms, or people just standing there, heads turned up as if they were listening to something, their faces seeming to float in the dark, lit by the fluorescent bars of the all-night lights.

22.

The Agony in the Garden Bar
Pete

The singer was a black woman who wore stretchy slipper-socks, discretely, along with her long, evening gown. She had arrived just yesterday, and she was to depart tomorrow, and her feet were swollen from sitting on planes. The singer lived in a kind of limbo of piano lounges all over Asia. Temporarily. She sang "Indigo Mood," and "Blue Moon," and "Somebody Loves Me" night after night in the best hotels for month-long travel stints twice a year. Then she went back to Kansas City and her voice students and steady work there with the opera and several jazz clubs, and to her husband Chuck, who was very understanding, and their eight-year-old son Max, who was bright for his age, well-adjusted, happy.

Pete didn't know any of this about the singer. He just thought of the singer as here—in the Garden Bar of the Pagoda, a hotel some distance from the Hotel New Riverview—pulling in breath and releasing it in such a way as to cause song.

Pete had listened to the singer from 9 to 11 p.m. every night of the trip, taking a cab to and fro. He came the first night in an agony of alienation. He had fled the Hotel New Riverview, declining an invitation from Keith to visit the hotel bar for a night cap. He was going nowhere, anywhere. The trip loomed as an ordeal; he was ill, hot and sweaty. The cab driver deposited him here, and he found a table, ordered his drink, and sat paralyzed with despair. There were few other patrons, for which he was grateful. He could sit and stare blankly, which he intended to do, steadily drinking Bloody Marys. He might never return to the Hotel New Riverview. He might never return to the Western Hemisphere. A therapeutic trip. That's what this was supposed to be. But he was dying. If not now, then later. If he wasn't already dead.

And then the singer appeared, this black woman in her long white gown. And he experienced a glimpse, just a hint that very first night, of a strange, temporary peace. The vision flickered, it came and went and came again over the course of the week, even as the irritations of the tour grew and the feeling that he was wearing down.

The absolute anonymity of this Garden Bar. To be expected, but unknown. Every night he returned to the bar, promptly at nine, leaving anyone in the world who had ever made his acquaintance, even very recently, far behind, and he and the singer and her combo were contained together in the time between the beginning of the first song to the end of the last.

He thought about the brass gongs at the temples the group toured all week. Sometimes there was just one big gong, sometimes a series of little ones. To strike them, the big one or all the little ones, one after another, was like praying, if he had it right. The prayer was the sound, and it lasted as long as the air waves oscillated, and that was that.

The singer knew Pete's face by now and she smiled "Hello" as she continued her first song. He hoisted his prosthesis out of the path of the waiter and hid it under the table. His pant legs were too short because the pants were too tight. He'd had to borrow a pair of Keith's microfiber Travelers after the boat fiasco, his only other pair lost in the hotel laundry after a Bloody Mary mishap. The pants were full of zippers and Velcro and whatnot, but there was no expanding them. Luckily, he'd managed to restore his shirt to a wearable state with the hair dryer in the hotel bathroom, Keith's own soggy clothes hanging all around. He was saving his other shirt for the plane. He wondered how Ron's immaculate apparel fared. That river was none too clean. Good that Ron managed to keep his sunglasses, which probably cost him something.

Pete finished his drink and formulated some descriptions he might once have attempted to offer to various people about the singer ("with her flowing gown and little slippers") and the blond, ruddy-cheeked trumpet player ("looking like a golf pro, except for the tux") and the large, stoic drummer ("handles those sticks like they are just regular household tools, socket wrenches and what have you"). But he didn't formulate a description of the handsome, extremely talented Asian youth who looked like a younger Ron with those precise features, and who rose up off the piano bench during his improvisations, during the long passages of dense chord changes, his face darkening, his expression a scathing glance directed toward any empty chair.

There were a lot of empty chairs. It was 9 p.m. exactly, the last night of the trip, the beginning of the first set, still fairly early. Pete was waiting for another drink to arrive. He hadn't formulated a description of the young piano player even for himself. And he would be afraid to describe him out loud, knowing (as he had learned), that to put words to things, people, feelings, could be dangerous for all sorts of reasons, not the least of which was the fact that it could be perceived to be as intimate an act as touching.

Pete could not predict, in the case of the piano player, what kinds of words might arise. He was careful not to stare, especially when accidentally caught in the path of that dazed gaze, the quick contortion of emotion, or maybe it was just a physical sensation that the piano player spasmodically revealed to the mostly phantom audience. (Pete had no idea how these musicians operated.) It was so disturbing to look at—that contortion, whether emotional, physical, or maybe even spiritual—and so impossible not to. Pete tried to keep his own face expressionless.

O . . . Thou . . . Who art unchangeable, Whom nothing changes . . .

The words of a prayer floated to the top of Pete's thought and mixed with the songs. This seemed to be happening these days. It was irritating, but apparently unavoidable. Maybe he was purposefully pulling the words up, grabbing at them for ballast of some sort, but he didn't think so. It would be nice if they were indeed something firm, yes, something to cling to, but they seemed to have detached from any great body of knowledge or fundamental truth and they were just drifting.

Somebody loves me . . . Who art unchangeable . . . Somebody needs me . . . Whom nothing changes . . .

The words swung slowly in his brain like seaweed.

His drink arrived, and he saluted the slender waiter. (Courtly older man with crutch. In control. Alone, but okay.) The waiter bathed Pete with his smile. Pete then, as usual, felt blessed. *May we find our rest and remain at rest . . .* He would leave a large tip under his water glass at the end of the evening . . . *in Thee, unchanging.*

~

Some of the priests he'd met in his day had been reading priests, adding a kind of developed philosophy, a useful psychology, to their life of prayer. They read in upright chairs, fully dressed, smelling of Irish Spring and Right Guard, their legs crossed, their pages marked with leather bookmarks from university bookstores or with silk-tasseled holy cards. They were evenly benevolent, putting their books down if interrupted and folding their hands over their knees to show they were listening. They called even the most irritating busybodies of the town "my child," given the appropriate circumstances, a death in the family, illness, maniacal behavior, breakdowns. They went on spiritual retreats together, they traveled to Assisi, they conducted guided tours through the Vatican.

These were the visiting priests, who appeared in small parishes only for short stints—"spiritual outreach," they referred to it, *Communitas,* they called it. They gave workshops in the parish basement, workshops that had fuzzy and foreign-sounding names—*Cursio, Des Colores*—they all had an upbeat spin. *Poverello* was the name for the teen ministry a visiting priest set up with the community Food Bank. The kids pronounced it like a pop song, flicking the "r" off their tongues, making hip-hop gestures, maybe joking, maybe not. ("Funiculi, funicula," muttered Pete.)

The visiting priests were trying to juice up the liturgy, Pete supposed, a move everyone seemed to appreciate except himself, who was not hip, nor hop, who felt this "outreach" as a tacit indictment of his own inadequacy and paralysis.

"Through my fault, through my fault, through my most grievous fault."

When Pete said Mass as Father Jackson, his neck glowed red with discomfort during most of the ritual and all through the torturous homily, when he had to try over and over, Sunday after Sunday, to interpret the themes of the gospel for his parishioners.

The Prodigal Son. *When the son of yours came, who has devoured your living with harlots, you killed for him the fatted calf.* What the hell was he supposed to make of that?

The Agony in the Garden. *The maid said to Peter, "Are you not one of this man's disciples?" He said, "I am not."*

He much preferred weekday Mass—no homily. And no crying babies. On weekdays there were only the muttered words, English, no longer Latin, but still detached from any construed meaning, performed almost privately, like the act of dressing, shrugging on the vestments alongside one sleepy altar boy, just morning ablutions, a pragmatic formula for putting one foot ahead of the other, just instructions, instructions for survival. On Sundays, though, he had to come up with some pious point to passages that he just wanted to leave alone.

Your brother was dead, and is alive; he was lost, and he is found. Fact. This happens. News update. End of story.

Are you a friend of Jesus? I am not.

Usually he filled up the allotted homily time by reiterating details from the bulletin. Persons whose names were on the Permanent Adoration List for Fridays should please call such-and-such a number. The Faith Formation In-service meeting would be switched to Thursday. The Strings of Tranquility, a new, non-denominational,

Hospice-affiliated ministry, had offered its services to all interested persons. (They'd better not get near *him* with their damn harps when he lay dying.) Extreme Unction kits (seldom requested these days), were available at the church office.

Sometimes he tried to bring the gospel to life by talking about the lack of rain and the bad harvest and the dangers of coveting this and that. He didn't know what else to say; he'd been a comic book kid himself, he had few references. His parishioner's eyes glazed over, they slept. Not once, in the thirty-odd years he'd been at St. Leo's had anyone ever commented on his homily.

The visiting priests (well, there had only been two, but they'd made an impact) went on various kinds of sabbaticals. They read Augustine's *City of God* on airplanes, saving Merton for the beach. They claimed to be engaged in postdoctoral studies, and did, in fact, carry around drafts of learned papers in their briefcases, which they insisted on sharing. "(Re)Visioning God's Archipelago," "Samsara: Christian Equivalences," "The Devil Made Me Do It: Aspects of the Concept of Evil as We Approach the New Millennium".

These priests might drive several hundred miles to attend a poetry reading by Sir Geoffrey Hill. (His voice, they cheerily reported, "had a seismic resonance, it rang like a death knell!") And then they indulged in educated repartee at the wine and cheese reception afterward. They began their homilies with an easy joke or two, just a tiny bit dangerous, somewhat disrespectful to the Pope. People sat up and laughed. These priests were secure. If they poked fun at the Vatican it was as insiders, team players with avid fans.

Why didn't they strap on a parish of their own? That's what Pete muttered to himself. The altar boys loved these visiting priests, who ruffled their hair and lightly smacked their ears, a fatherly display of fondness Pete had never mastered. The teen groups called these visiting priests "Father Tim" and "Father Paul." Slides were shown in the basement of the parish hall—slides of food distribution programs in Africa, or slides of these very priests marching for peace or nuclear disarmament, back in the day, arm in arm, wearing white shirts that gave a hint of the ecclesiastical, but no doubt bore some fancy little fashion logo. On Saturday afternoons they might listen to the opera on NPR, if it was Puccini, cutting it awfully close for the 5 o'clock Mass. They were insiders and world citizens, both, the whole ball of wax.

Pete was not one of these priests. Certainly, he knew the litany of the Mass like the back of his hand, in English and in Latin, and of course he knew prayers beyond the standard canon. Occasionally he tried to incorporate a snippet of scholarly wisdom into his homily—*When a man is virtuous enough to be able to delude himself that he is almost perfect, he may enter into a dangerous condition of blindness in which all his violent efforts finally to grasp perfection strengthen his hidden imperfections and* . . . The effect was uncertain. He became confused. The words hung heavy in the church, and he hurried to a close, as if he knew what he just had said.

No, he had never been a reading priest, nor a traveling priest, nor a retreating priest, nor an educated/activist/outreach/sabbatical priest. He had not been fashionably mannered nor fashionably dressed. He had been a small-town kid, a bike-riding boy, just a regular guy who had grown up into the wrong vocation.

When he was thirteen there had been an accident. Nothing like this damn boat thing, a quick and fluky moment, then a lot of embarrassing hullabaloo. His accident had not been like that at all. It had happened out on the prairie, empty, unwitnessed, on an oil pump, of all things, he had tried to ride the big oil pump as if it were a horse. He'd never ridden a horse, never mind an oil pump. He was a townie, for Christ's sake, he just had his crappy bike.

He had been alone. He had envisioned telling the other junior high boys about this feat and then taking them all back to the pasture to show them, do it again. He had imagined the junior high girls being amazed at his free-wheeling spirit, his innovative hijinks. His pants became caught in the mechanism, predictably enough, and he lost most of his lower left leg before falling off his "horse" and nearly bleeding to death. A rancher checking fences found him.

It was the only thing out of the ordinary that had ever happened to him.

He was marked by that moment on the prairie, made different. But it was his deformity that everyone talked about, not his dazzling behavior. He was marked, made different, and he mistook this for a call. He was like Saul, he decided, Saul become Paul, he'd learned the whole story in catechism class. How Saul had been struck off his horse and turned into a saint.

Pete couldn't bear the thought that he'd simply been maimed. He was just a kid, starting out! But no basketball, no football, no military, no love, probably, or so he decided at age thirteen. All right, he'd be chosen then, called to a life in Christ. He wanted companionship, he wanted to be on a team of some sort. So, okay. Chosen. Picked! That's what he decided. But he was wrong.

For nearly forty years Pete was a rock, just like Peter the apostle. He said Mass, heard confessions, baptized babies, visited the sick, gave last rites, buried the dead. He did all this with loneliness living in his throat. His parents died, his sister moved away. He performed the holy sacrament of matrimony, counseling the young couples about abstinence and fertility, the rhythm method, struggling with the words, his face red. He briefly had a cat, which ran away. He tried to talk about love at meetings of the high school CYO, the Catholic Youth Organization, those meetings where he was asked to address a topic, about once a year. He tried to relate love to the passion and death of Christ. The kids frowned. They whispered and passed each other notes. He got a dog, but it got run over.

He told the kids to call him Father Pete, but they never did.

"You can call me The Rock," he tried that as an alternative, going for a joke. "Like the apostle, not the wrestler!" The young people looked at him, their eyes expressionless. It took him almost forty years (forty days and forty nights and forty days and forty nights and...) to realize that he did not have a vocation. He had not been called at all. He had misheard.

He watched the news at six, got the mail at one, and endured the long Saturdays of January, three goddamn clocks ticking in the rectory, the reading priests probably at ski retreats. (No "outreach" for *them* on the northern plains in winter.) They probably said Mass at high country chalets, served as in-house chaplains for weeks at a time at upscale resorts or on cruise ships, counseled at-risk rich kids. Those visiting priests knew other priests who had left the priesthood to marry. They knew priests who devoted themselves full-time to academia. Themselves, they got fellowship-type deals to go live in Rome.

Pete hung on. He just hung on. Then he let go and fell.

The prayers had been given to him at certain points, literally pressed into his hands, and they sank straight to the bottom of his soul upon receipt, laden as they were with the concern and caring of their deliverers, the poorly-paid substance abuse counselors, the drably-dressed lay nuns. They were weights, not anchors, these prayers. They didn't secure him so much as drag him down.

Thou art moved... But the words, lately, had become unmoored, lightened, released... *in infinite love*... They had undergone a strange surfacing. They'd lifted from the floor of his emotions and they floated closer now to the top of his heart, his brain, his soul, inching their way up toward the outer edges of the world. *The need of a sparrow*... They were rising as he dissipated, he supposed... *even this moves Thee*... They rose as he grew sick... *A human sigh, this moves Thee*... Sick and old.

O, infinite love.

He was a golfing priest. Out there at the Chokecherry Country Club, along the wide Missouri, the air thin, sometimes warm, always windy, the course lovingly coaxed from the sage and dry prairie grasses, watered daily except during droughts. He thought of golf as a kind of ministry (or so he sometimes told himself), he and the rest of his foursome working their way around the course like saying a rosary, and afterward, if it was a weekday, not Saturday, and he didn't have to get back for the 5 o'clock Mass, and the others were taking time off or playing hooky from their jobs, there might be a sweaty *Communitas* in the clubhouse, all eighteen holes rehashed with good-natured jibing, and on some holy days there was drinking until dusk.

Golf was like saying a rosary, drinking was like golf. Created, crafted, measured. You were on a mission, you grasped your task right in your hand. You lived inside the cup.

Most times the others went home to their families, to wives and children and dogs, bikes in the driveway, hot showers, the phone all tied up, eating out on the deck, work the next day, bed early. Pete went home to the rectory. On Fridays, Saturdays, and Sundays, when Mrs. Schmidt had her days off, he microwaved things she left for him. Except for all the clocks, the rectory was silent.

When he golfed, he used a cart and a cane, left his crutch in the car, and—until he was disgraced, transferred, then put out to pasture, "de facto defrocked," as he thought of it, "given the papal boot," in short: deep-sixed (a stay in the Brother's House, or some such thing, on offer, but not anything practically helpful, like, say, detox)—he had been moderately admired in the town.

He hung on, he just hung on. Year after year. Then he let go. And it had been so sweet, the feeling of connection, so briefly, intensely, sweet. He did not believe in God, he finally knew that. But suddenly, after years and years, he had again felt marked, made different. Made whole, this time, as if he were pulled back up onto his oil rig "horse," a passive action on his part, a relinquishment, a rising, an ascension, an action in reverse. He rode the horse again and felt the boys and girls of junior high cheering. He felt the redemption of his long, maimed life. He did not believe in God. But in an instant, all at once, in the quick touch of fingertips, flick of an eye, he believed in God's love.

A young man, a boy, barely fourteen, one boy out of the many years' collection of cold-eyed teenagers. A boy who wore his dark hair long, just like this piano player. Pete didn't touch him, not beyond the quick once. He just looked at him, often, and one day the boy looked back. He gave to Pete a flash of understanding, a glow of light.

There is color in the fall. Pete tried to stay steady in the face of accusations. He had done nothing, there was no sin of either commission or omission. Just a reverse, somehow, of his long affliction. That's how it felt to him. A redemption, yes, you could call it that. I'm redeemed! He wanted to shout it. But in everyone's eyes he saw: You're at fault.

He tried to maintain, stay steady, take it as it came. He even attempted to craft a prayer of sorts as he packed his bags to leave St. Leo's. His kiss-off gift was this guided tour—the visiting priests had intervened at his crucifixion, "Retracing Merton's Path in Asia" the suggested goal. The itinerary, to Pete, looked like some description of several levels of hell, Merton's tragic end implied. But his distant sister somehow got into the act, so he finally said Ok, all right.

Looking out his window at the glittering coins of the quaking aspen, poised to swirl to the ground, he packed his bags and prayed. *There is color in the fall.* That was his prayer, and it held some consolation. Fact. *There is color in the fall from grace.*

~

The singer winked at Pete, her smile like a warm rain.

The slender waiter placed a dish of rice crackers next to his drink (O, Love . . .), and the young piano player scowled through a long improvisation that seemed to be especially full of suffering, passion, anger, forgiveness.

Anyway, beyond words.

23.
O, Infinite

Ron was having trouble keeping everyone corralled at the airport. They needed to pay a $10 airport tax in US cash or the equivalent in local currency. He already had told them that. He had reminded them several times. Nevertheless, half of the group scattered in search of an ATM machine, while the other half became distracted by the very first gift shop inside the sliding doors, where they were buying little bags and bells and other souvenirs, Mrs. Small adding a particularly lacy fan to what had become a collection.

Denise said she planned to load up on Shiseido products at the duty-free shop; she had her Mom's American Express card at the ready. But first she napped in a chair, her closed eyes free of mascara after her early hour shower, making her look much younger and rather boyish in her bib overalls, a little frown denting her tattoo. A Hindu woman in a brilliant blue sari with a red jewel between her eyes smiled slightly as she contemplated Denise.

"Do you believe in the unity of the individual self with the universal self?" Mr. Small posed this question to Ron. He was reading from his philosophy book. Mrs. Small nudged him along, and he batted her away with his free hand. He wanted to get in a last-minute Buddhist discussion. He'd had a lot of coffee. He told Mrs. Small that he would be most obliged if she would keep track of their place in the check-in line while he figured out the mind of Man.

"Man is man because of man," said Ron, sighing deeply and look-ing at his watch. "And woman," he added, glancing at Mrs. Small, who was now employing her passport to hurry Mr. Small.

"You enjoy philosophy," the elderly man with the bolo tie informed Mr. Small.

"Philosophy is like homesickness, an urge to be at home every-where," responded Mr. Small. "I quote the poet Novalis."

"That's a good one," said the old man.

~

Irene planned to buy two liters of Gordon's at the duty-free shop. She didn't have to worry about hauling the weight around; she was connecting at SeaTac to another plane flying right on to Crag, where Melvin would meet her. It was several dollars cheaper than at Wylie's Spirits, and she didn't care who saw her buy it, she wouldn't be seeing these people anytime soon, if ever. Unless, of course, the Smalls were serious about her coming to visit them in Seattle. They'd discovered in the course of conversation that she lived near an Indian reserva-tion, which they said they found fascinating. Ever since learning that fact, Mr. Small had paid more attention to her and Mrs. Small had quizzed her about the problems of alcoholism.

"Is it just rural areas in general, or Native populations per se?" Mrs. Small was bringing it up again.

"Rural areas and urban areas, but restricted to men and women," Pete answered for Irene.

"Sometimes a small amount of gin will ward off a cold," Irene offered, and Pete nodded his agreement.

The elderly man with the bullet bolo tie commented that Monica was missing.

"Where is Monica?" he asked around, calling her by name, then clarifying with reference to her bracelets. It turned out that she was down in a part of the airport rarely seen by the common traveler. It was called the Quarantine Area, and it was where her carry-on bag was languishing, waiting for her to claim it. She mistakenly had left it in the hotel lobby during the groggy departure, and it had arrived separately, via the hotel van. When Monica finally appeared—her absence having inspired an actual, muttered "Gawd dammit" from an unsmiling Ron—she and her bag looked equally dusty and dented. Monica's disarray had an ethnic cast to it, garbed as she was from head to toe in patterned cloth with lots of embroidery. She had befriended representatives from a number of hill tribes over the course of the week and reported that she was able to buy things not normally sold at any of the markets. She was juggling a stack of wide-brimmed hats made from palm and banana leaves, as well as several hand-painted masks, and there was a wild look to her eyes.

"Get in line, get in line, goodbye, goodbye . . ." Ron was inspired to one last incantation as he gestured toward the security personnel, using his collapsed umbrella as a subtle prod, trying to launch them into the No Man's Land of the interior airport zones, where he could only hope they'd find their gate.

Holding one of Monica's painted masks to his face, his hand on his hip, Ron struck a brief pose, a joker or a court jester. Continuing to motion with his umbrella for them to move along, he held the mask in place. Keith was slowing down the proceedings by insisting that Ron repeat aloud Keith's mailing address, which Ron did, the words muffled.

"Take off your face!" Keith laughed.

Ron reached out and handed the mask over the cordon to the frowning Monica, who was nearly at clearance, and she placed it on the conveyor belt behind Sterling, who was slung face down. Ron then abruptly said his goodbyes, waving perfunctorily, nodding to the security personnel, turning on his heel and leaving at a hurried clip, glancing at his watch again, his smile obscured, then gone.

Keith watched him go. When he said goodbye, he had quickly taken Ron's hand and clapped him on the back.

Keith and Pete finally had established a little golf talk, then there was the dunk in the river and subsequent lending of clothes, though not a great deal in the way of "thank you" from Pete. After the singing on the boat, Alfred had struck up a conversation with Keith, letting him know that he participated in a men's choir back home. But Ron was the fellow Keith would remember. The fellow he would miss.

He wanted to hug him, but he didn't.

~

The giant plane detached from the earth with a reluctant spring. It was chased into the sky by its own roar.

Off we go! Into the wild, blue, yonder! (Herbert was soundlessly singing.)

At just that moment another plane, smaller, a domestic flight headed for a popular island gambling resort, crashed into the ocean twenty-seven miles off the coast, killing everyone on board. The members of the RealRoutes Chartered Quests PARADISE PROM-ISE SuperValue Tour to Amazing Asia! would not learn of this until several days had passed and they all had returned to normal.

"That could have been us," Iris would suggest to Alfred. "But it wasn't."

~

Keith looked at his breakfast tray. He loved this little doll food, the plastic knife and fork wrapped up with a miniature napkin like a party favor. Someone sliced these oranges and arranged them just so with the parsley. They sliced them and arranged them and then went home to their own mysterious corner of the world. They never thought of Keith, nor he of them, not really. But someone, nevertheless, sliced these oranges and arranged them for Keith, just so, with the parsley.

"A heavy mist obscured the scene."

Ever since the boat accident the elderly man with the bolo tie had been telling hero stories involving water, his voice projecting above the plane's drone. At first it was swimming water, then it turned into drinking water.

"'Water! Water!' they cried. But there was none to give."

The in-flight movie was *The Truman Show*, starring Jim Carrey, a comic actor, but it wasn't a comedy. Half of the group watched Jim Carrey as he tentatively, fearfully, touched the sky. He had thought that the sky was just air and that it went on and on. But it was, in fact, a big bubble-dome, some sort of painted canvas. There certainly had been a number of these sorts of movies lately, Mr. Small remarked to Mrs. Small. What's real, what's not, is it now or not at all, somebody's dream, TV, or *what*? Mrs. Small took Mr. Small's hand and tucked it into her lap.

The elderly man speculated about the makeup of the sky to the student from Hong Kong who had become his chosen audience.

"Maxwell S. Elgar," the man introduced himself to the student when they first were seated. Neither of them opted to rent headphones, but they'd been keeping an eye on the video screens. Perhaps the sky was plastic or maybe some kind of tarp. It wasn't real, anyway, at least not really a sky, and there the fellow had been the whole time, trapped inside it. The student smiled uniformly at every comment made by Maxwell S. Elgar, who, losing interest in the movie, resumed his hero stories.

"'They want water?' the youth asked. 'Water they must have!'"

Jim Carrey poked his hand at a long rip in the blue above him, astonished.

"Both friend and foe would tell of this brave deed."

Maxwell S. Elgar finished his story and then held up his hand in a time-out gesture while he had a fit of coughing.

Irene explained the movie to a couple from Indiana, even though the couple had rented headphones and were engrossed. She was thinking of writing a travel article about making conversation on an airplane. It would be called "The Neighbor to Your Right." She was making herself practice on the couple.

The character's entire life had been inside a bubble-dome, Irene explained. It was all just a show for other people, who watched him

on TV, and he never knew. Irene's voice was getting excited and over-
loud. She was pleased with herself for picking up on this strange
aspect of the movie. But whether it was marvelous or not (a question
Mr. Small posed to her from across the aisle, when the couple was
unresponsive), she was not sure. Was it terrible that the sky turned
out to be fake and finite? Irene wondered this silently while searching her purse for a cough drop. Or, as Mr. Small speculated, was the
character glad? Glad to have something to break?

Jim Carrey stepped through the sky to the other side.

Half of the plane napped. Alfred and Iris wore eye masks, purchased at the airport at Keith's suggestion. Even asleep, they looked
self-conscious.

"Such acts are worthy of the pride of men and angels."

Maxwell S. Elgar was wrapping up a whole other story, quoting
obscurely. The student from Hong Kong chuckled and said "Yes, okay."

~

**You will cross the International Date Line and arrive home
on the same day.**

When we land, we'll wake up and wonder where the hell we've been.
Denise was very tired. Somehow, a fat, placid baby sat on her lap.
The baby looked at Denise questioningly, wheezing a bit. It smelled
a tad ripe. *Go to sleep,* Denise said with her eyes, *we're all going to
sleep now.* The baby exhibited a delighted interest in Denise's tattoo,
touching it gently with a sticky finger and then smiling a wide, jack
o' lantern smile, showing one tooth. Denise had offered to hold the
baby while the parents (a horror show of disorganization, in Denise's
opinion) got settled. Then she just kept it, the parents beaming on.
The baby was heavy, pinning her to her seat, a lump of warm humanity. She smelled the yeasty wisps of hair. They smelled good, or at
least familiar.

The plane reached an elevation of 32,345 feet. The pilot drawled
that they were now in the jet stream. Denise could hear Keith com-

menting loudly to anyone who cared to listen that the jet stream was just like a river way up high in the atmosphere. It was invisible, Keith continued, but it was there. It was a kind of current that cut through the blue, carrying them over the globe, faster, faster.

Acknowledgments

Many thanks to the editors and staff of the following presses and journals for first publishing excerpts of this novel, sometimes in different forms:

"M(r). Butterfly" originally appeared in *Salon* magazine, February 4, 2000.

"Funny Blood" was a semi-finalist in *Carve* magazine's Raymond Carver Short Story Contest for 2016, and appears in *Bright Bones: An Anthology of Contemporary Montana Writing* (Open Country Press, 2018).

"The Aliens Among Us" won an honorable mention in the 2016 Rick DeMarinis Short Story Contest of *Cutthroat, a Journal of the Arts*, and appears in *Truth to Power: Writers Respond to the Rhetoric of Hate and Fear* (*Cutthroat, a Journal of the Arts*, 2017).

"Into the World" appeared as "As We Waft Out Into the World," in *Salon* magazine, May 12, 2000.

The Virginia Center for the Creative Arts provided space and time for the completion of this book. I am grateful for this support.

I would like to thank my Aunt Alice and Uncle John. Their engagement with the world has always been an inspiration to me, and the guided tour they invited me to join inspired some parts of this writing. We were travelers together, though none of us—nor anyone we personally know—appears here.

Megan McNamer grew up in northern Montana and studied music at the University of Montana and received an MA in ethnomusicology at the University of Washington. *Home Everywhere* (Black Lawrence Press, 2018) is her second novel. Her first novel, *Children and Lunatics* (Black Lawrence Press, 2016), won the Big Moose Prize. Essays and stories have appeared in *Salon, Sports Illustrated, The Sun, Tropic Magazine* (of *The Miami Herald*), *Islands Magazine, Headwall, Cutthroat Magazine,* and a number of anthologies, and have won awards from *New Millennium, Glimmer Train,* Writers@Work, the University of New Orleans Writing Contest for Study Abroad, Travelers' Tales Best Travel Writing Solas Awards for 2016, and *Carve* magazine's Raymond Carver Short Story Contest for 2016. Megan lives in Missoula, Montana and plays Balinese music with the community gamelan Manik Harum.